"I got a call from the stalker today."

A sharp intake of breath as Mac leaned forward was his only reaction. Pretending his nearness didn't affect her, she relayed the conversation.

"Are you sure that was wise? What if this person has grown more unstable? What if she's dangerous? You know she said you would pay."

"I've always known this person is unstable."

Agitated, as much by how badly she wanted to touch him as she was by the situation, she jumped from her chair and began to pace.

"Why do you think she'd be breaking in to my house and calling me?"

A muscle worked in Mac's jaw. "Yo── realize you are putting yourself in dang───

Swallowing hard, she bold── ──t's time to end this, once ────── ─g on you to keep me

Dear Reader,

Losing someone is difficult and painful. I can't imagine losing my spouse and then almost immediately after, my child. But that's what Mac Riordan goes through when his wife is killed in a car accident and their newborn baby is stolen from the hospital. He will stop at nothing to find his son and get him back.

Loving someone means wanting what's best for them. And when Mac finds the child he believes is his with a woman who clearly loves him, how can he rip the boy away from the only mother he's ever known? Add a pinch of danger from someone else who believes the child is hers and you have an emotional story fraught with danger.

Writing this story was a lot of fun. I adored exploring the various emotions of Mac and Emily as they dance around each other, learning to trust, daring to dream, hoping to love. And when danger threatens all they hold dear, watching as they joined ranks to protect the little boy they both love was thrilling and inspiring.

I hope you enjoy reading *The Cop's Missing Child* as much as I enjoyed writing it!

Sincerely,

Karen Whiddon

KAREN WHIDDON

The Cop's Missing Child

HARLEQUIN®

entertain, enrich, inspire™

Recycling programs
for this product may
not exist in your area.

ISBN-13: 978-0-373-27789-6

THE COP'S MISSING CHILD

Printed in U.S.A.

Books by Karen Whiddon

Romantic Suspense

The CEO's Secret Baby #1662
The Cop's Missing Child #1719

Silhouette Romantic Suspense

★*One Eye Open* #1301
★*One Eye Closed* #1365
★*Secrets of the Wolf* #1397
The Princess's Secret Scandal #1416
Bulletproof Marriage #1484
★★*Black Sheep P.I.* #1513
★★*The Perfect Soldier* #1557
★★*Profile for Seduction* #1629
Colton's Christmas Baby #1636

Harlequin Nocturne

★*Wolf Whisperer* #128

Silhouette Nocturne

★*Cry of the Wolf* #7
★*Touch of the Wolf* #12
★*Dance of the Wolf* #45
★*Wild Wolf* #67
★*Lone Wolf* #103

★The Pack
★★The Cordasic Legacy

KAREN WHIDDON

started weaving fanciful tales for her younger brothers at the age of eleven. Amidst the Catskill Mountains of New York, then the Rocky Mountains of Colorado, she fueled her imagination with the natural beauty that surrounded her. Karen now lives in north Texas, where she shares her life with her very own hero of a husband and three doting dogs. Also an entrepreneur, she divides her time between the business she started and writing. You can email Karen at KWhiddon1@aol.com or write to her at P.O. Box 820807, Fort Worth, TX 76182. Fans of her writing can also check out her website, www.karenwhiddon.com.

To my family, because they are above all the most important part of my life.

Chapter 1

The bright sun felt warm on his skin. If he'd been here for no reason other than a desire to enjoy the weather, Mac Riordan would have stopped and turned his face up to let the bright rays try to heat blood that these days always seemed chilled. Instead, he glanced around while keeping his quarry in sight, taking in the lush greenness of the park crowded with citizens enjoying the early spring air.

He couldn't believe the hunter's rush he felt at this planned-for encounter. Finally, after all this time, he'd meet the woman who had, inadvertently or not, stolen everything he had left to live for.

He'd planned this carefully, just happened to take a stroll along the tree-lined, paved walking path when the very woman he'd come to town to find strode past him on her daily walk—Emily Gilley. He'd been watching her for a week, after all, and figured an accidental meeting in the park would be a great way to meet her.

True, if he wanted this to appear unintentional, keeping up with her confident pace without looking as though he was stalking her might prove difficult, though not impossible.

He doubted she'd find him suspicious. From what he'd heard about the east Texas town of Anniversary, everyone was friendly and trusting and looked out for each other. If this was true, then Emily Gilley would have no reason to worry about a friendly stranger.

He allowed himself the slightest of grim smiles. If only she knew.

So far, he'd been careful. After all, he'd only been in town for three weeks. It was just long enough to establish his brand-new trucking business and to put out a few feelers about her, the woman he'd spent several years trying to locate: Emily Gilley, twenty-nine-year-old widow of one of the most notorious drug dealers on the Eastern Seaboard. She'd changed her name, taking back her mother's maiden name Gilley, and altered both the cut and the color of her hair, all to help her disappear. But for someone with the far-flung resources to which he had access, finding her had been a matter of time and a tenacious effort. He was fortunate to still have a lot of the tools from his law enforcement days at his disposal.

Her long, blond locks were now dark, short and spiky. Instead of designer fashions, she wore clothing that looked off the rack at a big bin department store. She'd gone from a glamorous life in Manhattan to this: a tiny lakefront community ninety miles east of Dallas.

As he hurried around a bend at the end of the trail, trying not to appear in too much of a rush, he nearly ran into her. She'd stopped at the weathered wooden bench that marked the entrance to the paved parking lot of Sue's Catfish Hut, which was crowded with lunch-time patrons.

She was stopped and turned to face him, apparently willing to wait for him to catch up.

This was going even better than he'd hoped, he thought with some satisfaction. And then he got a look at her annoyed expression.

Hands on her hips, she glared at him, her brown eyes full of anger mixed with only the barest hint of fear. "What do you want? Stop following me! If you're trying to creep me out, you're succeeding admirably."

He dipped his chin, sending her an abashed smile he hoped she'd find reassuring. "My apologies. I had no idea this was a private trail."

Instead of growing flustered, she shook her head, sending her shaggy spiked hair rippling. "It's not. But I walk here every day on my lunch break, and I know almost everyone in town. Every time I look up, you're right behind me. You never pass me or fall back. And while this is the first time I've seen you here, you have to understand how such behavior can make a woman feel threatened."

"Threatened? Interesting choice of words." He crossed his arms. "I'm new here, and I mean you no harm. I wasn't aware being a newcomer and taking a walk were crimes."

Narrowing her eyes, she studied him, apparently not buying his too-easy, confident patter. In his experience, overly suspicious or outright paranoid people usually had something to hide. But then again, she had a point. He was a stranger who was following her, and her for-mer husband had been a drug dealer. No doubt, looking over her shoulder had been deeply ingrained in her psyche. She'd be foolish not to worry. And one thing he'd learned about Emily Gilley, formerly Cavell, was that she was anything but stupid.

Finally, she took a deep breath, exhaling it slowly.

"Look," she said, her tone reasonable this time rather than furious, "you've been following me way too closely. What matters is that you've made me very uncomfortable." Swallowing hard, she studied him, her caramel gaze unflinching. "And even though this is a small town, one can't be too careful."

It was especially true for a woman like her, with so many secrets to hide.

He nodded, feigning chagrin. "Again, I apologize. If I'd known I was frightening you, I would have dropped back or—" he grimaced ruefully "—I would have tried to pass you."

Rather than accept his apology, she straightened her shoulders and lifted her chin. "You said you're new in town, right?"

"Yes." Relieved and slightly surprised that getting to know her was going to be this simple, he gave her a practiced, easy smile, holding out his hand. "Mac Riordan."

Instead of a handshake, she simply continued to stare him down. Only when he'd dropped his hand and frowned did she speak again in a cool, measured tone. "Welcome to Anniversary, Mac Riordan. I don't know who you are or what you want, but in the future, please leave me alone.

Tamping down shock, he feigned confusion instead. "Ma'am, I—"

Backing up slightly, she tilted her head and peered up at him. "Let me ask you something. Are you the one who mailed me the note? It was postmarked Dallas. Is that where you're from?"

"Note?" He eyed her warily. Had someone tipped her off about his arrival? "What note? I have no idea what you're talking about."

"You didn't send me an anonymous note? Cut out letters on white paper?"

Was this a joke? Then, as he realized what she'd said, his former cop instincts made him ask, "Is someone sending you threatening notes?"

Again he got the sharp, brown-glass stare, as if she thought if she tried hard enough she could read his mind. Since he'd been looked at all kinds of ways by all sorts of people in his previous life in law enforcement, he let her. Silence was often the best interrogation method of all.

"You didn't answer my question. Are you from Dallas?"

"No," he fired back. "Albany, New York. Now tell me about this note."

"That's none of your business," she said calmly, her spine so rigid he thought it might snap. Then, apparently considering he might in fact be harmless, she swallowed, still eyeing him warily.

"I'm sorry. I didn't mean to be so rude. I've got to go." She mouthed the words, sounding anything but. Without another word, she marched off, her spiky dark hair ruffling in the breeze.

Watching her slender, lithe body as she went, he couldn't help but respect that she knew enough to be wary. Because if their situations had been reversed, he'd have done exactly the same. People on the run from former lives couldn't afford to befriend curious strangers.

This was exactly the reason he had to make sure he gained her trust—no matter what it took.

Even as she hurried away, Emily Gilley felt the tall, dark-haired stranger's gaze boring into her back. She felt flushed and hot, though not entirely from her brisk walk. Instead, she worried about the man with the striking cobalt eyes. At first glance, the tinge of gray in his hair had made him look older by at least a decade. But up close, his rugged face appeared to be only a few years older than she. Mid-thirties, perhaps, a handsome, muscular man who moved with easy grace. Any other woman would have been intrigued by his blatant masculinity, his self-confident virility.

Not she…she knew better. Sex on the hoof didn't last past the morning, and men like him were nothing but trouble. After all, she'd been married to one once.

This man singled her out. Why? She couldn't help but wonder if this attempt to appear older was deliberate, an effort to camouflage who he really was—or *what* he was.

He was a threat. She couldn't believe his sudden appearance the same day after getting her first threat since moving here was a mere coincidence. How could it be?

The unsigned note that had appeared in her mailbox that morning had been similar to the ones she used to get back in New York. Letters cut and pasted from a magazine, the three sentences read exactly like the ones she'd received before. Her stalker—and Ryan's, for the note always mentioned her five-year-old son by name—had somehow found her here, in an innocuous small Texas town.

This meant it was time to move on.

She considered, suddenly exhausted by it all, she could run again. Or she could stay—and fight.

Because quite frankly, she liked living here in Anniversary, Texas. She'd made friends, and while her receptionist job at Tearmann's Animal Clinic wasn't glamorous, she loved the sheer ordinariness of it. All in all, she'd made a cozy home for herself and her son here.

Damned if she would give that up without a battle. She'd paid enough for crimes she hadn't even committed. Never mind that she'd been completely clueless about her husband's nefarious activities. A lot of people thought she should still be held equally responsible, especially now that Carlos was dead.

Without any idea why, she'd always assumed the threatening notes had come from one of Carlos's mistresses. She knew of two, and there'd probably been more. Any one of them could have viewed his death as a breach of promise and his wife as the rival who got everything—especially since Emily had always suspected one of those women had been the one to birth her son and give him up for adoption, no doubt at Carlos's urging. She could only hope he hadn't forced the issue, which would mean there was another woman out there mourning the loss of her son.

Even though Emily could definitely sympathize if that was the case, she was Ryan's mother now, and she'd made a good home for him here. The only thing she wanted to do was pretend her former life had never happened. All she'd brought with her from that life was her son. He was all that mattered.

Hurrying from the walking trail and across the parking lot to Sue's Catfish Hut, she refused to look over her shoulder at the man. She sensed him still standing where she'd left him, watching her. She could feel his gaze burning into her back.

"Afternoon, Letty." Lifting her hand in a friendly wave to the elderly cashier, Emily slid inside the empty booth. She spent quite a few of her sixty-minute lunches exactly the same way—a brisk walk around the park and then a bite to eat at Sue's with her friend Jayne Cooper.

"Hey, lady." Jayne plopped into the seat opposite her. Jayne's normally frizzy blond hair had been tied back in a ponytail. She worked in the police station down the street, one of three dispatchers. "Who was that man you were talking to in the park? He looks like that new guy who moved here from up north somewhere. I can't remember his name."

Surprised, Emily tensed and then forced herself to relax. Good grief, she was tired of being suspicious of everything and everyone. She'd honestly believed she'd gotten over that, until the stalker's note timed with the appearance of the strange man had brought all her old fears back to life.

"He said his name is Mac Riordan. He said he's new in town."

"That's right, he is." Snapping her fingers, Jayne nodded. "Everyone in the sheriff's office has been talking about him. Apparently, he and Renee Beauchamp go way back. He moved here a couple of weeks ago and opened a trucking company. He bought the Stamflin place out on FM 3356."

Emily simply nodded. "So he's legit then?"

Now Jayne studied her closely. "As opposed to what? Some crazed serial killer? You are the biggest worry-wart I know."

Somehow, Emily managed to effect a careless shrug.

"That comes from living in Manhattan. You can't be too careful there."

As Jayne was about to speak—no doubt to launch into her favorite topic, the bliss of bucolic existence in Anniversary—their friend Tina appeared with two tall glasses of iced tea. "Here you go, ladies. Are you both having the usual today?"

"Yes," Emily and Jayne answered in unison.

"Good." Grinning widely, Tina winked. "I already put in the order ticket. Lord, help me if you ever decide to walk on the wild side and try something else."

Just then, the front door opened, and the noisy dining room went abruptly quiet for a moment before the noise level resumed. Emily's heart sank. Mac Riordan's large frame filled the doorway and he scanned the room.

When his gaze connected with hers, Emily tensed, resisting the urge to duck under the table. Just because the man decided to have his lunch at the same place didn't make him her stalker. Right?

"Oooh, my," Jayne breathed. "Emily, honey, why didn't you mention that he is absolutely gorgeous?"

"You saw him in the park."

"From a distance, Em. Only from a distance."

"Emily? You know him?" Tina asked sharply.

When Emily shook her head, Tina narrowed her heavily made-up eyes. "You're blushing," she pointed out. "Why is that?"

Blushing? It was true that her face felt warm, but Emily never blushed. "I just met him a few minutes ago in the park, that's all," she said, aware she sounded as if she was trying too hard to be casual.

"Uh-huh." Clearly believing there was more to the story, Tina nodded. "I'm calling an immediate lady's night this Friday. Mexican food and margaritas. I can't wait to hear all about this."

"There's nothing to tell," Emily began. "I…" The words caught in her throat as Mac began slowly making his way toward her booth, drawing the gaze of every busybody in the restaurant—in other words, just about everyone.

Jayne and Tina grew wide-eyed as he approached them. Idly, Emily wondered why it seemed every woman in the restaurant appeared to be drooling, then pushed the thought away.

Her skin prickled as he dipped his chin at Tina, then Jayne, before facing Emily. "I'd like to have a word with you, if you don't mind," he said in a quiet yet authorative voice.

"I'm about to eat lunch," Emily told him firmly, refusing to look at either of her friends, though she could feel them staring in astonishment.

"Fair enough. How about after?"

Most of the other patrons in the restaurant made no attempt to hide their avid eavesdropping. Slightly desperate, Emily hesitated. She hated to think that this one chance encounter could undermine all of her attempts to fit in this town.

"Fine," she finally said, just to make him go away. "Now please, let me eat my lunch in peace."

For an answer, he dipped his chin again, then moved away to take a seat at the bar. She couldn't help but notice he'd chosen his stool with care, claiming the one closest to the front door so he could stop her if she tried to make an escape.

"Well, well, well," Tina said. "I think there's a lot more to tell us about than a chance meeting in the park."

The kitchen chose that moment to ring the bell, signaling Tina that she had an order up. Relieved, Emily watched her go, aware she'd been temporarily spared from answering. Not that there was anything to tell, though she knew her friends would never believe that.

As Tina left to fetch their lunch, Jayne regarded Emily curiously. "Are you all right?" she asked. "You look a bit pale."

Keeping her hands under the table so her friend wouldn't see her wringing them, Emily frowned. "I don't understand why he wants to talk to me. I've already said everything I need to say when I ran into him in the park."

"Which was?" Jayne prompted.

"Basically, to leave me alone."

"Wow. Way to win friends and make enemies."

"Oh, come on." Irritated, Emily eyed Tina making her way toward them with their lunch. "You would have done the same if you'd been walking alone and some man started following you."

Jayne shook her head, dislodging pieces of her ponytail. "Sweetie, he's drop-dead, to-die-for hot. What's wrong with you?"

"And he followed me relentlessly. Even in here. Tell me you don't think that's weird."

This prompted Jayne to snort inelegantly. "That kind of weird is like a gift from heaven. I mean, look at him!"

Tina reached their table and set down their catfish in front of them. "Here you go, girls. Have you noticed every single woman in here is eyeing your Mr. Tall, Dark and Handsome?"

"He's not mine." Picking up her fork, Emily stabbed a corn bread hush puppy with her fork, popping it into her mouth to discourage further questions. As she chewed, she studiously avoided looking in the direction of the lunch bar.

Jayne and Tina had no such compunction.

"Well, if you don't want him, mind if I have a try?" Tina finally drawled, her east Texas twang as thick as syrup.

"Go right ahead," Emily answered once she'd finished chewing. "Just be careful he doesn't murder you in your sleep."

"Emily!" both women chided.

"You've got to get over that paranoia." Shaking her head, then her hips, Tina sashayed away. Emily picked at her food, her appetite gone.

"You really are upset about this, aren't you?" Jayne asked, taking another bite of the crisp golden fish.

"I'll be fine." Her automatic answer, made even now to a woman she counted among her friends, meant she wasn't. But her self-protective instincts, awakened after the craziness that had followed her husband's death, refused to stay dormant for long. Experience had taught her nothing was ever as it seemed.

"Are you going to talk to him after we eat?"

Emily took a long drink of her iced tea. "I guess so. Hopefully, I can convince him to leave me alone."

"Maybe he just wants to ask you out on a date."

Emily's forced laugh told her friend what she thought of that idea. "No. He doesn't. Believe me."

From her expression, Jayne clearly didn't. "Do you want me to come with you when you talk to him?"

Surprised and grateful, Emily touched the back of Jayne's hand. "No, but thank you for offering."

The sympathy in Jayne's eyes made Emily's throat close up. Trying to regain her equilibrium, she stabbed a piece of fish and forced herself to chew it.

"Sometimes you remind me of Rocco," Jayne said. "When we got him from the Boxer rescue, he was terrified of every move we made."

At her friend's analogy, Emily had to smile. "You're comparing me to your dog?"

"Believe me when I say that's the highest compliment I could pay you. It took Rocco six months to begin to trust me. I've known you four and a half years, and I still wonder if you'll ever stop being shocked at the kindness of others," Jayne mused. "I know you don't like to talk about your past, but you seem to be wound a bit too tight. If you ever need someone to lend an ear…"

This line of conversation, while hardly new, had the potential to go on for hours. Over time, she'd told both her best friends about her past, at least the part before Carlos. Unlike Ryan, she hadn't been fortunate enough to be adopted. Due to poor health and a variety of childhood diseases, she hadn't even been shuttled from foster home to foster home. Instead, she'd spent her childhood in an orphanage, venturing out into the world alone as soon as she turned eighteen. She'd met Carlos shortly after that, and the whirlwind courtship and marriage had seemed exactly what she'd needed.

Ah, the naivete of youth. Emily checked her watch. She had ten minutes left before she had to return to work.

Tapping her watch face and shaking her head at her friend, she ate a couple more bites of her fish before blotting her mouth with her napkin.

"I've got to go, or I'll be late," she said, tossing her payment on the table.

"What about him?" Still eating, Jayne jerked her head in Mac Riordan's direction. "You told him you'd talk to him. And since you can't get out the door without going past him…"

Though she already knew the time, Emily made a big show of checking her watch once more. "I hope he can make this quick and painless."

Still, despite her misgivings, her mouth went dry the closer she got to him. Mac stood as she approached, placing his money on the counter and falling into step with her as they headed out the door. Though her heartbeat immediately started racing, she kept her face expressionless and waited until they'd emerged into the bright spring sunshine before speaking.

"All right," she told him. "I work down the street, and I have five minutes left on my lunch break. What do you want?"

Instead of answering, he took her arm. Immediately, she tensed, causing him to drop his hand. He shot her a look but didn't comment on her defensive body language.

"Let's walk and talk," he said.

Without responding, she set off at a brisk pace for the vet clinic. She hated the way she felt hyperaware of him, hated the way a single glance at him made her insides go all weak and warm.

When they'd covered half the distance without him telling her what he wanted, she finally stopped and turned to face him. "Why do you need to talk to me?" Though she spoke in a soft voice, she made sure a thread of steel ran through it. "I don't know you, and I'd like to keep it that way."

"You mentioned a threatening letter," he began.

"I never said it was *threatening*." Despite the alarm bells clanging inside her head, she still felt an insistent tug of attraction.

"Cut out letters? Come on. Why else would you ask if I mailed it to you?" he said in a reasonable tone. "I'm new in town, and we've never met before today, so that's the only way your question makes sense."

Put that way, he sort of had a point. But his supposed concern didn't excuse his odd behavior. At one time, she would have allowed herself to feel flattered. Now she could only feel threatened. "Look, you've been following me. First on the walking path, then you came into the restaurant and made a public scene."

Now he tilted his head. "That was not a scene. I have nothing to hide. Do you?"

She shuddered, unable to conceal her reaction. "If that's not creepy, stalkerish behavior, I don't know what it is. So I'll ask you one more time, what do you want?"

"To help you."

"Of course you do." Unable to rein in her sarcastic response, she crossed her arms. "Out of the goodness of your heart, right? You don't even know me. And I sure as hell don't know you."

"Cop instincts, I guess. I used to be a detective in the Albany Police Department. Your sheriff's department can vouch for me."

Wearily, she nodded. Jayne had said something of the sort. "You still haven't told me what you want."

"I'd like to offer my services," he said, his gaze steady.

"No, thanks." She shook her head.

"For a fee, if that will make you feel better. If you need protection, I can help."

Dumbfounded despite herself, Emily looked away. Whatever she'd expected him to say, it hadn't been this. The idea of having help of some kind—any kind—felt so seductive that she nearly swayed with relief.

But she didn't…because she knew better. Despite his movie-star good looks and the tug of sexual attraction she felt when she looked at him, she couldn't afford to trust him. She couldn't allow herself the luxury of letting her guard down. The sins of her husband's past were too numerous.

"Look, I appreciate your offer." Softening her voice, she tried to appear as if she meant it. "In reality, I had a couple of blind dates with a guy who liked me way more than I liked him. I'm pretty sure that's all this is."

Devilishly handsome, he studied her. With his hawk-like features and his too-sharp blue eyes, everything about him spoke of inherent strength. Ah, but she knew better than most how appearances could be deceiving.

"Give me his name, and I'll talk to him," he said. "If it is him, I'll make sure he doesn't bother you again."

She recoiled, unable to help herself. Her late husband had been such a man, promising to take care of her, keeping her shielded from the rest of the world. At first, she'd found this charming. It wasn't until later that she'd realized she'd been slowly suffocating.

And when she'd found out her entire marriage, her entire life had all been nothing but a pack of lies, she'd known she shouldn't have been surprised. But she was. And hurt and betrayed. She'd vowed she'd never be so blind again.

This was why, even though this man's rugged profile made her want to melt inside, she wanted to play it safe and send him away—with a smile, if possible.

Because the last thing she needed was to make another enemy. God knows she had made enough of those already, thanks to Carlos.

Chapter 2

Careful not to flash a confident smile, Mac waited for Emily to accept his offer. Though he'd never been anyone's bodyguard, he felt he'd do a superb job. Being a former cop had its advantages.

"No, thank you," she said instead and then turned and hurried inside Tearmann's Animal Clinic, leaving him standing alone on the sidewalk. Scratching his head, he grimaced, wondering why he'd even thought this would be easy. Years of experience should have taught him that nothing ever was.

Turning, he headed back toward the parking lot where he'd left his pickup truck. The other day he'd been talking to his friend and former partner Joe, who still worked for the Albany P.D. Joe had speculated that someone like Emily Gilley was a chameleon. She could change everything about herself to suit the place and the occasion. Now that he'd met her, Mac thought Joe might be dead-on accurate about this.

He'd have to regroup and replan. His quarry was nervous and wary—and rightfully so. He'd been watching her from a distance ever since he'd arrived in Anniversary. Despite the time he'd put in learning about her and her routine, he'd yet to catch a glimpse of Ryan, the boy she passed off as her son.

This, he vowed silently, would become his number one priority.

Heart pounding and hands shaking, Emily walked over to the front desk, summoning a smile for Sally, the gum-chewing redhead who covered the reception area every day while Emily had lunch.

"You look like you've seen a ghost. Are you all right?" Sally asked, tilting her head and peering at Emily with concern.

"I'm fine," Emily lied, managing a limp smile. "It's kind of hot outside, and I think I got kind of dehydrated, that's all."

Immediately, the older woman's frown cleared. "I'll bring you a bottle of water from the back." She hurried off, leaving a trail of strong perfume in her wake.

As soon as she was gone, Emily sank down in her chair. She fought against instinct—the urge to run away, to quit her job, drive home immediately, pack her and Ryan's things and get the hell out of Texas. She wanted to run…again…away from anything she perceived as a threat…away from him.

She took a few deep breaths. Sally returned, bearing the promised water. As Emily opened her mouth to speak, the phone rang. Waving her thanks to Sally,

Emily answered, keeping her voice steady and professionally polite.

After she completed that booking—a morning spay—some clients came in: the Jones family with their three pugs. After that, a steady stream of phone calls and customers kept her busy. Somehow the afternoon flew by without her once thinking about Mac Riordan and the danger of his beautiful, casual smile.

Finally, the last appointment left and Emily locked the front door. She rushed through her normal closing duties, straightening the waiting room magazines and making sure the front door glass was smudge free. If she hurried, she'd make it to Mim's Day Care where her son attended the after school program half an hour before closing time, and she and Ryan could swing by the grocery store and pick up the boxes of macaroni and cheese she'd been promising to make him, along with his beloved hot dogs, for supper.

The next morning, Emily woke with a renewed sense of purpose. She refused to allow herself to be run out of town. She just had to figure out the best way to fight. Sure, Mac Riordan was handsome and a charmer, but Carlos had been the same. She knew how to deal with men like him, even if it meant pushing away the simmering attraction she felt for him.

Feeling strong, she went to wake Ryan.

She sat down on the edge of his rumpled bed and watched him sleep, her heart bursting with love. As usual, seconds after she touched his shoulder, her son opened his eyes wide and held out his arms from a hug. Her throat clogged and her eyes filled as she wrapped her arms around him, breathing in the shampoo scent in his clean hair.

"I love you, mama," he murmured, his voice full of sleep and sounding younger than his five years.

She cleared her throat, smiling mistily. "I love you too, Ryan."

As she poured him cereal, a good compromise between the sugary one he'd wanted and the totally healthy one she had chosen, she found herself taking comfort in the familiar routine. No matter what kind of day she had at work, sharing her mornings with Ryan and looking forward to the evening ahead kept her motivated to have a positive day.

After breakfast, she followed him to his room to check out his clothing choices. Once she'd approved those, which happened more and more often these days, she grabbed the car key, buckled her son in his car seat and left.

"Have a good day." Leaning down to kiss her squirming son's cheek, she breathed in the apple juice and soap scent of him and wished the knot in her chest would ease.

"I will." Ryan shifted from one foot to the other, clearly eager to hurry inside his kindergarten classroom but equally loathe to abandon his mother.

"Go on, then." She gave him a tiny push, smiling as he tore off without another glance at her.

Looking at her watch as she left the elementary school, she waved at Mrs. Parsons, the assistant principal who always took morning duty at the front door, before hurrying to her car. The small gray Honda had been old when she'd purchased it, but it was clean, dent-free and it ran well, which was all she cared about. Every day she had to get Ryan to school and then pick him up from day care after. That, combined with her job and weekly trips to the grocery store, didn't seem to be more than the little car could handle.

Now though, she had one more errand she wanted to run before she had to be at work. Emily planned to pay a visit to the sheriff's office. One thing she'd learned being married to Carlos had been that the squeaky wheel got the grease. If she didn't push, she knew they'd ignore her worries over the anonymous letter. They had no idea of her life story and the reason she took such things seriously, and if she had her way, they never would. That said, she had no intention of ending up one of those horrific stories you see on the evening news.

She'd make sure the Anniversary Police Department viewed her threatening letter as…well, as threatening as she did.

Already in her office, Renee Beauchamp looked up as Emily approached. Though her brown eyes appeared bright, the faint dark circles under told a different story.

"Good morning," Emily said firmly, stepping into the sheriff's office uninvited and taking a seat in one of the two chrome-and-cloth chairs facing the desk. "I'd like a moment of your time."

Renee nodded, her expression showing nothing but professional interest. "What can I do for you, Ms. Gilley?"

"I'm here to find out what you've learned about the letter." Another trick Emily had learned was to state things as though they were fact, rather than ask questions. This conveyed both a sense of confidence and of purpose.

"Nothing, actually." Renee steepled her fingers on the desk in front of her. "We've had very little to go on, and since there was no specific threat—"

"Oh, but there was," Emily interrupted firmly. Pulling her copy from her purse, she read the relevant line. *"I know what you've done. You've stolen what is mine and you'll pay for what you did. Tell the truth, or risk everything."*

Nodding, Renee leaned forward. "While I appreciate and understand your concern, the letter is too vague. If, for example, it read 'I'm going to plant a bomb in your garage' or something, we'd have cause to act. But the wording 'you'll pay' conveys nothing."

Biting back an instinctive response, Emily swallowed back her anger. Just because the sheriff spoke factually didn't mean she didn't have a private, visceral reaction. As a woman, she must. Emily knew she had to appeal to this if she wanted help.

"Do you have children, Renee?" Emily asked softly.

A quick shadow appeared in Renee's eyes, then vanished. "No, I don't."

She held up her hand as Emily opened her mouth to speak. "But that doesn't mean I don't get where you're coming from."

"Then how can you tell me it's not a threat?"

"Because the letter did not directly threaten you or your son," Renee said gently. "And if you read it again, you'll see there is absolutely no specific threat in there—at all."

Incredulous, Emily had to force herself to close her mouth. "You honestly don't believe 'you'll pay for taking him' puts me—or him—in any danger?"

"Ms. Gilley—"

Bulldozing through whatever platitude the other woman was about to offer, Emily stood. "Ryan is adopted, Renee. I know you had no way of knowing that, but I can't help feel this letter is somehow related to that."

A tiny frown appeared between the sheriff's perfectly arched eyebrows. She sat up straighter, giving Emily a piercing look. "All right. I'll check it out. I'll need to ask you a few questions."

"Of course." Emily watched while Renee grabbed a pen and pad.

"Did you go through a service, or was the adoption privately arranged?"

"It was private." Emily managed to sound confident. "My former husband—I'm a widow—handled everything. But I located all the records he gave me back then and would be glad to provide you with copies."

"I'd like that." The sheriff stood, holding out her hand. "Just bring them by at your earliest convenience."

Standing also, Emily shook hands. It was almost time for her to head to work. "Thank you. I will."

"Have a good day."

"Oh, I have one last question." Turning in the doorway, Emily tried for both a casual expression and carefree voice. "What do you know about Mac Riordan?"

To her surprise, Renee laughed. "He's an okay sort of guy. He's new in town, and I don't know him that well, though my friend Joe speaks highly of him. Mac used to be a cop, up in Albany, which is where Joe works. I heard Mac kind of spooked you a bit."

"He did, a little." With a cheery wave and a manufactured smile, Emily let herself out, sighing. The damn letter had succeeded in erasing nearly four and a half years of security, all at once. Mac Riordan's appearance had made things even worse. After all, Albany was only several hours north of Manhattan.

She didn't just have her own security to worry about.

She had to keep her son safe. Clearly she had a decision to make—and quickly.

Once at work, Emily pushed the letter from her mind...and Mac Riordan, as well. Though as her lunch hour approached and she prepared to head out for her daily walk, she couldn't help but think of him. Surely he'd taken the hint and wouldn't show up in the park today.

If he did, she'd have to accept that he was stalking her. And then she'd have to quit her job, pick up Ryan and go home and pack, running away in the middle of the night without a single goodbye to anyone.

Heart pounding and feeling queasy at the thought, she shook her head. Maybe if she tried to think logically, it was possible the man simply liked her. She'd felt a sort of electrical connection, despite having all her barriers up. From the way he'd looked at her, blue eyes dark and full of promise, he'd felt it, too. Exhaling, she laced up her sneakers and nevertheless prayed he wouldn't be there.

He wasn't. The pressure in her chest and the sick feeling in her stomach eased a little as she enjoyed a quiet, uninterrupted walk. The sun shone brightly; a few white, fluffy clouds dotted the sky like sheep; and birds sang, dogs barked, and people all around her enjoyed the bright spring day.

After, perspiring slightly and feeling pretty good, she stepped into Sue's Catfish Hut and greeted her friends. As she took her usual seat, she couldn't help but do a quick scan of the restaurant for a sight of those broad shoulders and dark gray hair.

Again, Mac Riordan was conspicuously absent. For the first time all day, she allowed herself to relax, even though a tiny part of her felt disappointed at his absence. She enjoyed her meal, chatting with Jayne and Tina and sipping iced tea.

She went back to work with a light step, allowing herself to believe everything just might turn out to be all right. By the end of the workday, she felt almost normal.

After helping close up the veterinary clinic, she hopped in her car and headed over to the day care.

As soon as she arrived, Ryan flung himself at her, holding on to her legs with a fierce grip.

"Finally," he groused. "It took you forever to pick me up. I'm all played out."

She couldn't help but laugh at his choice of words. The after school programs at Mims's Day Care tended to lean toward organized games, most of them physical. The tall trees made the heavily shaded playground the perfect place for youngsters to run off pent-up aggressions or simply play.

"Well, now you get to rest," she said. "Grab your stuff and we'll go."

He did as she asked, snatching up his camo backpack and waving goodbye to his friends.

Once she'd buckled him into his booster seat, she climbed in the front and started the engine.

"How's a tuna casserole sound for dinner?" This should be a sure hit since he always loved the one she made, using the leftover mac and cheese from last night and adding a can of peas and a can of tuna.

"No. I want a Good Times meal." Looking mutinous, little Ryan crossed his arms and lifted his chin. "With fries. No tuna."

Tired as she might be, still Emily managed to summon a smile for her son. "Rough day at school?" she asked, leaning over the backseat and ruffling his hair.

"Yep. And at Mim's, too. I'm tired of playing."

This was a new one. "Tired of playing? You? Why?"

"Because they always make me be the bad guy."

Emily blinked. "Really? Why?"

He looked away, his lower lip quivering. "I dunno. Mommy, can we please get a Good Times meal?"

Though she'd planned on making the casserole and eating it for a couple of days, she relented. "Sure, I guess I'll just get a salad or something."

Apparently everyone's children wanted Good Times meals. The drive-thru line had six cars already waiting. Emily debated going inside, but judging from the crowded interior, she'd be better off waiting in her car—especially since Ryan kept fidgeting, whining and protesting he was too big for a booster seat, even though the law stated he had to weigh a hundred pounds before graduated to just being buckled into the seat belt.

"You've still got some growing to do," she informed him.

"I haven't been weighed lately," he said huffily. "Now I'm a big boy. I bet I weigh a hundred and five now."

Considering him solemnly, she somehow kept from smiling. "Okay," she finally said. "When we get home, we'll check."

He pumped his little fist up in the air. "And next time I go in the car, I can buckle up like a big person?"

"If you weigh over one hundred." Which she knew he didn't.

"And I can ride in the front with you?"

"We'll see." Finally, they reached the window. Placing her order, she glanced back at her son, who'd finally fallen quiet. He was staring at something in the parking lot. As she followed his gaze, she recoiled. Mac Riordan stood next to a large white pickup truck, talking to another man. As far as she could tell, he hadn't seen her.

Struggling to hide her fear, she handed the money to the window cashier, accepted her order and put the car in Drive. Heart pounding, she pulled away, using only her rearview mirror to make sure she hadn't been spotted.

All the way home, jumpy and unsettled, she kept checking to make sure they weren't being followed. Nothing out of the ordinary occurred, and they pulled into the driveway slowly.

Not for the first time, Emily wished she could afford an automatic garage door opener. How much simpler and safer it would be to just hit a button, pull into the concealed garage and close the door behind you, all before even getting out of the car.

If she stayed in Anniversary, she'd have to put money aside to buy one.

Parking, she gave the rearview mirror one final check before unlocking the doors. The smell of fast-food made her stomach growl, and she was glad she'd opted for a grilled chicken sandwich instead of a salad. She needed something a bit more substantial today, especially since she knew she wouldn't be getting much sleep.

Making decisions had never been her strong suit. She literally had to force herself to act at times—especially if she didn't have a clear picture of potential repercussions.

She wished she could be one of those kinds of people who could go with their gut, trusting their instinct. Not her...she always required the facts.

Helping Ryan out of the car, she took his hand. Together, they walked up the sidewalk to the front of their circa 1960 rental house. Then she realized something was wrong.

"Hold on." Grasping Ryan's hand firmly, she stopped. "Don't move."

Though she'd locked it securely that morning, the front door was slightly ajar and obviously unlocked. Someone had been—or was still—inside her house.

Chapter 3

Since Emily wouldn't hire him as her bodyguard, Mac knew it was time to go to plan B. He sauntered into the Anniversary Police Department, intent on asking Renee for a job. To his surprise, she sat at the front desk in the receptionist's chair, typing up something on a decrepit manual typewriter.

"You got a minute?" he asked.

"Sure." Pinning him with her direct gaze, she dragged a hand through her short hair. "Perfect timing, Riordan. I've been meaning to call you and ask you to come in. Follow me," she ordered, jumping to her feet and giving Mac a hard look as though she thought he might run off.

When they reached her office, she took a seat behind her desk and indicated he should sit in what he thought of as the suspect's chair...interesting.

Taking a seat, he leaned back, crossing his arms.

He'd let her go first, since obviously she had something on her mind.

In typical cop fashion, Renee got right to the point.

"How well do you know Emily Gilley?"

"I've only met her one time, in the park." It was a truthful answer—especially since Renee didn't need to know about all the research Mac had done to find her, and more importantly, to find Ryan.

"You seemed very interested in her."

He spread his hands. "What can I say? She's a pretty lady." Again, he only spoke the truth.

Renee seemed to sense this—or at least, he hoped she did. "You know, Riordan, I'm just doing my job. I actually believe you."

"Good to know." He allowed a slight smile. "I did offer to be her bodyguard. She turned me down flat."

Staring, Renee narrowed her eyes. Then, apparently deciding he was serious, she dipped her head, grinning. "I should tell you that I ran a check on you and talked to your former partner back in Albany. Joe and I go way back. He had nothing bad to say about you."

It was unsurprising. Joe was his best friend, and Mac had been a very good police officer. He would still be, if he hadn't left his job. But Joe had understood that finding Ryan had become more important to him than anything else.

"And on top of that," Renee continued, "Joe put me through to your lieutenant. Just like our mutual friend Joe, your former boss speaks very highly of you."

"Good to know." Aware of his precarious position, he debated whether or not now would be a good time to broach his proposal. On the one hand, if Emily and Ryan were in serious danger, then he couldn't afford to wait. On the other, he didn't want to do anything that would make Renee even more suspicious of him.

To his surprise, Renee broached the subject for him. Dragging her hand through her cropped blond hair, she tapped her pen several times on her pad of paper. "Emily's scared. I'm beginning to think she might have a good reason to be. Unfortunately, we're really short-handed here."

Though her words kick-started his heart into over-drive, he held himself perfectly still and merely nodded.

Appropriately encouraged, she continued. "I know you have a trucking business to run and all, but would you consider coming to work for me part-time? Like a few hours a week?"

While he pretended to consider her offer, she tossed out what for him clenched the deal. "I'd really like you to handle the Emily Gilley case exclusively."

A thousand thoughts raced through Emily's mind. First and foremost, she had to keep her son safe.

"Don't move," she repeated.

"But I'm hungry," Ryan started to whine, raising his face to hers. Something he saw in her expression must have gotten through to him, because he instantly went silent.

"What's wrong, Mama?" he whispered, his blue eyes huge in his small face. "Is everything okay?"

No, everything was not okay—though she didn't say that out loud to her five-year-old. "I don't know yet," she said instead, moving them backward. "I think we need to get back in the car and call the sheriff."

She wouldn't panic. She couldn't, even though she knew if her front door was open that someone had been in her house.

Backing out of her driveway, she drove to the corner gas station and mini-mart and parked.

"Go ahead and start on your Good Times meal, honey," she told Ryan, handing the brightly decorated box back to him. "Remember, no toy until you finish your meal."

She waited until he was happily munching away before taking a deep breath and pulling her phone from her purse.

Keeping the doors locked and the engine running, she made the call. When she asked to be put through directly to Renee, the dispatcher immediately did so—yet another difference between living in a large city and a small town.

Speaking quietly and calmly so she wouldn't alarm Ryan, she told Renee what had happened. "I didn't go inside," she said. "I have no idea if anyone is still in there."

"That's a wise move," Renee said. "Where are you now?"

Emily relayed her location.

"Stay put. We'll meet you there in less than five minutes," the sheriff promised. "The car will be an unmarked cruiser. No lights or sirens."

"All right." Disconnecting the call, Emily shoved her phone back into her purse and eyed her sandwich. It now looked wilted and completely unappetizing, though probably due more to the circumstances than the actual appearance. Even the thought of trying to eat made her stomach roil.

Law enforcement pulled up just over four minutes later, the unmarked Chevrolet still looking official and police-like. It was not Renee, Emily realized, but another officer, which was unusual since the Anniversary Police Department was so small.

Squinting, Emily tried to make him out. The passenger door opened, and a familiar dark-haired, broad-shouldered man emerged. She squinted, certain she wasn't seeing correctly. But as he approached, she realized that Mac Riordan, while not decked out in a crisply pressed navy police uniform, wore a police badge pinned to his button-down shirt.

As he walked toward her car, she was struck once again by the way he exuded masculinity. He was one of those men who, with one glance at their steely gaze, could make a woman feel safe and protected.

Foolishness, she chided herself. Nevertheless, her mouth went dry as he approached. Mac Riordan looked…different. She waited in silence until he reached her.

As if he sensed her confusion, he gave her a reassuring smile. "I'm working for the sheriff's office part-time. Renee asked me to handle your case."

Stunned, at first Emily didn't know how to respond. "But—"

Interrupting, his rich voice washed over her like waves in a storm. "I can assure you I'm completely qualified. I spent ten years at the Albany Police Department, working my way up from patrol to homicide detective."

"I'm sure you are," she said faintly.

Relief warring with trepidation, she opened her door.

But as she started to get out of her car, Mac waved her back.

"I want you to follow me, all right? I'm going to ask you to remain in your car while I make sure your home is safe."

Swallowing hard, Emily nodded. She had to be careful to hide any evidence of fear from her son, who watched the exchange with wide, curious eyes.

"Why are the police here, Mommy?"

Putting the car in Drive, she again checked her mirrors before pulling away. "Because I think someone might have been inside our house, honey."

He cocked his head, apparently unable to decide how to take this news. "A bad person?" he finally asked

"Maybe." She shrugged, as if this was not important. "We have no way of knowing. That's why we're letting the police check this out first."

"Maybe it was a bear!" Giggling, Ryan made a roaring sound. "Or maybe a deer got inside like that video we watched on the computer one time."

Thank goodness for his vivid imagination and his innocence. "Maybe," she allowed, even though there were no bears anywhere near their part of the country, unless one counted the bears living in the Dallas Zoo. "I guess we'll just have to wait and see."

"Can we take a video of our own, Mommy? Pleeeease?"

"We'll see." She gave him a reassuring smile, just in case he sensed her jangled nerves. "Let's wait until we find out what exactly got inside, okay?"

Nodding, he resumed playing with the little plastic airplane that had come with his meal.

An eternity passed, but finally they reached her street. The police car pulled into her driveway, and Mac motioned to Emily to park in the street one house down. She did as he asked, unwilling to take any chances with her son's safety.

Heart in her throat, she watched as Mac got out and headed toward her house. As he went around to the backyard, Emily turned around to distract Ryan, not wanting him to notice that Mac had drawn his gun.

"Let's go ahead and eat, honey," she urged watching as he tore into his Good Times meal.

While he ate, she alternated between keeping an eye on him and watching her house. Trying to will her heartbeat to slow down, she took a tiny bite of her grilled chicken sandwich. Chewing what tasted like ashes, she managed to choke it down and swallowed hard, setting her food aside.

Ryan had finished his burger and half his fries and was already restless. "Mommy? What is the policeman doing inside our house?" he asked, squirming in his seat. "Can we go inside yet?"

About to answer, she spotted Mac heading toward her car, his large form making her feel ridiculously safe. "Just a minute, sweetheart."

Rolling down the window, Emily peered up at the handsome man, trying not to hold her breath. "Well?"

"You've been burglarized," he said grimly. "Though I can't tell for sure what they were after. Your TV, stereo and computer were all untouched."

"Jewelry, maybe?" A lot of the more valuable pieces in Emily's collection had been given to her by Carlos, so she wouldn't mind too badly if they'd been stolen. After all, she had renter's insurance.

"I don't think so," he answered, his professional expression warring with the heat in his blue eyes. He glanced once at Ryan, then quickly back to her, keeping his gaze fixed on her face.

"Is it safe to go inside?" she asked, hating the note of breathlessness that had crept into her voice and hoping he put it down to her being upset about the break-in.

For an answer, he opened her door. "Come on. The

house is clear. I'll have you take a look, but glancing quickly through your things, it doesn't appear the intruder touched anything."

"Then why—" Emily started to ask, then looked down, reeling in shock. Suddenly, she *knew* exactly why the intruder had been in her home.

When she raised her head again to meet Mac's gaze, she hoped her expression was calm. "In my office—" she began, ignoring his proffered hand and climbing out of the car.

"What about me?" Ryan asked, fumbling with his seat belt. "I wanna go, too."

Emily glanced at Mac, receiving a nod of confirmation that it was safe. He seemed to be making a studious effort to avoid looking at her son, which, since it made no sense, was probably a figment of her imagination. "Of course you can come. We're home, after all. We're safe here." She emphasized the word *safe,* so Mac would not say anything unduly alarming within Ryan's hearing.

"Good." Her five-year-old sounded unfazed, cheerful rather than frightened. He jumped out of the car, landing on both feet with a solid *splunk.*

"Hey, there," Mac said from behind her, making her start slightly, which Ryan noticed. When he looked up, he saw the unfamiliar man for the first time. Pulling on her leg, her son tried to disappear behind her.

"Honey, it's all right," she soothed. "This is Deputy Riordan. He's here to help us find out who broke into our house."

Ryan peeked out from around her leg. Glancing from her boy to the man who now crouched down to put himself at Ryan's level, she was surprised to see a look of naked, awful pain on Mac's craggy face.

She was about to ask him what was wrong but forced herself to hold her tongue.

"Go ahead and say hello to the nice policeman," she urged softly.

Holding himself rigidly, her brave little boy eased out and around her and then held out his hand. "I'm Ryan Gilley," he said politely, exactly as she'd taught him.

Gently taking the small hand, Mac swallowed hard as he shook it. Again, she realized he appeared to be in the throes of some deep, strong emotion, which made her wonder if she'd been right, and he'd actually lost a child.

"Pleased to meet you, Ryan," Mac finally said, his voice husky. "I like your backpack."

This was exactly the right comment to make. Ryan had spent hours searching for the perfect backpack. He'd ignored the popular cartoon characters and chosen a green-and-tan camouflage material pack. When she'd asked him why, he'd told her he wanted to be a hunter when he got older. Since he wouldn't even harm a spider, insisting she carry it outside rather than squishing it, she couldn't imagine that ever happening, but let it go.

"Thanks." Glancing up at Emily, Ryan edged closer. "Come on, Mommy. I want to make sure nobody stole any of my toys."

Exchanging a quick glance with Mac, Emily nodded and held out her hand for Ryan to take. He did so and then began tugging on her, clearly in a hurry to get inside the house.

Stepping into her living room, Emily stifled a gasp. The place hadn't been merely burglarized—it had been trashed. It was torn up, tossed around and destroyed on purpose. Though Ryan continued to pull her in the general direction of his bedroom, she couldn't help but slow and try to take in the sheer scope of the damage.

"Hang on a minute, Ryan," she said sharply. "Stay here with Mommy while I look around."

About to protest, Ryan glanced from her to the sheriff's deputy and nodded instead.

While she stood, trying to take in the scope of the destruction, all she could think of was to be thankful she and Ryan hadn't been home. She could clean up the mess, replace whatever had been stolen, but if anyone had harmed her son... The very thought made her shudder.

Wordlessly, Mac came up beside her, placing a hand reassuringly on her shoulder as if he knew her thoughts.

Instantly, she jerked away. "Where's Renee? I'd really hoped—"

"You do want to find this stalker, right?"

Emily stiffened. "Of course. It's just—"

"I'm assigned to your case. And I'm good. I promise you that I will find this guy."

The brief urge that had her wanting to lean against Mac appalled her. She nodded, wondering why she had such a strong, adverse reaction to him. It wasn't as if the man had actually done anything to warrant her mistrust and suspicion—well, aside from following her into Sue's Catfish Hut the first time they'd met. Maybe it was her persistent, instantaneous attraction to him.

Could she trust him? Did she even have a choice?

Aware both he and Ryan were watching her expectantly, she forced a pleasant, if humorless, smile. "All right. Why don't you tell me what you're going to do about this?"

Spreading her hands to encompass the total trashing of her home, she realized she was perilously close to tears. That knowledge alone was enough to cause her to shore up her shoulders, take a deep breath and lift her chin.

"We'll find the guy," he said simply. "I promise you that."

"Thank you." She hoped he didn't notice the catch in her voice. Glancing down at her son, who now seemed engrossed in playing with the toy that had come with his Good Times meal, she sighed. "What now?"

"Take a look around and see if anything is missing," Mac said, his deep voice rolling over her in a wave of calmness.

The sick dread in the pit of her stomach refused to leave, but Emily forced herself to head toward the room she used as an office. Luckily, this was right next to her son's bedroom.

"Mommy!" Ryan crowed, tugging his hand free and catapulting onto his bed. "They didn't touch my toys!"

After a quick inspection of his room, including under the bed and in the closet, Emily left him happily playing with his trucks and went to check out her desk.

"They were looking for something among your files," Mac said quietly behind her. File folders and paper were strewn all over the desk, chair, foldout couch and floor.

A manila folder sat open and empty on top of her desk. Before she even picked it up to read the label, Emily knew what it was.

"Ryan's adoption records," she said out loud. "They stole Ryan's adoption records."

Spinning, she grabbed Mac's arm. "You've got to help me. Whoever broke in here is after my son. You've got to help me protect him."

Mac's sharp blue gaze searched her face. "Do you have other copies?"

"Of course." Punching the on button, she powered up her computer. "I scanned them and saved them, both here and on CD."

"I'd like copies."

"Of course." As soon as the computer booted up, Emily clicked on the folder and printed them off, handing them to him.

"Was anything else taken, besides your son's adoption paperwork?" he asked.

"Not that I can tell." Twisting her hands together, she tried to sound unaffected.

"Let's check the rest of the house," he said. Without waiting for an answer, he turned and went down the hall to the next bedroom—Ryan's room.

It, she reflected thankfully, appeared untouched. Oblivious to his mother's chaotic thoughts, Ryan cheerfully played with a couple of his trucks, ignoring the adults.

Mac paused at the doorway, watching silently, as though the cheerfully untidy mess was more than he'd expected.

"Do you have children?" she asked softly.

He started, as if her question had brought him out of deep contemplation. "Currently, no." His abrupt tone made it sound like the topic was both painful and closed.

"I'm sorry." She shrugged, suddenly feeling uncomfortable again. "Please excuse the mess. Ryan's only five, which is why—"

"No need to explain." His back to her, he stepped into the room the way one might enter a church. Again, she cursed her overactive imagination. There was no logical reason why a man—a sheriff's deputy and experienced police officer—would act in such a way.

Unless…

She blinked. Though she didn't know him well enough to ask, again she wondered if he'd lost a child.

"Was anything taken from here?" he asked, directing the question to her rather than Ryan.

"No," Ryan answered, without looking up from his trucks. "All my stuff is okay."

"Thanks." Flashing her son a reassuring smile, he moved close to Emily and spoke in a low voice. "Would you mind taking a quick look around and letting me know if you see anything missing? Just in case?"

"Of course." Horrified at the thought, she took a step forward, trying to mentally catalog Ryan's toys. After a preliminary sweep of the room, heart in her throat, she looked at Mac helplessly. "Honestly, he has so much. Do you really think someone would—"

"Probably not." He touched her shoulder, the gentle grip meaning to reassure her. "After all, your stalker seems more concerned with you and the adoption than with your son himself. I'm sure there's nothing to worry about."

They were good words, but the idea of someone taking one of Ryan's toys like some kind of trophy opened up an entirely new world of terrifying possibilities. Again, she felt the strong urge to gather her meager belongings, pick up her son and run as fast and as far as she could.

"Emily?"

Realizing Mac had been talking to her, asking her something, she forced herself to concentrate on him. "I'm sorry," she said. To her surprise, she sounded relatively normal. "What did you say?"

"I asked you if you could walk with me to the other rooms."

With her heart skipping a beat, she couldn't help but glance back at Ryan. Loath to leave her son, conversely she didn't want to alarm him.

"He'll be fine," Mac said. "Let him play."

"Just a couple of bathrooms and the laundry room."

He stepped into the hall and gestured. "Lead the way."

Heartbeat far too rapid, she headed for the hallway and her bedroom, with Mac following. While she'd begun to think Mac Riordan might be an okay kind of guy, something about him still felt a bit off, though she'd be hard-pressed to specify exactly how.

He searched her room first. She noted how he moved with a brisk efficiency, treating her home and her belongings with respect. Appreciating that, she felt the tightness in her chest begin to ease somewhat.

When they'd finished, they wound up back at the front door. "Is that it?" she asked. "Is there anything else you need?"

Considering, Mac cocked his head. "Now that we've finished checking out your house, I have a few questions. I'll need a minute or two of your time."

"You've got it." Though she knew he wanted to ask her about her past, which normally would have caused her to shut down completely, she also realized she'd need to answer honestly. Otherwise, there was no possible way on earth that this small-town sheriff's department could even remotely understand what they might be up against.

Making an instant decision to tell the truth, though not all of it, Emily led the way to the kitchen. "Have a seat. I'm guessing this might take a while."

"That depends on how much you have to tell me." When Mac's humorous tone failed to produce an answering smile, he grew serious. "Why don't you start with what you know was actually taken? Why Ryan's adoption records?"

She considered her words carefully, an actual ingrained habit since she'd chosen this way of life.

"I was married to a…criminal." Wincing as an expression of understanding filled Mac's sky-blue eyes, she held up her hand. "No, it's not what you think. I didn't know about him until after he died. My husband is dead."

"I'm sorry to hear that. Did he die of natural causes?"

No one but a cop would have thought to ask such a thing. "No." She debated whether or not to elaborate, then realized with a bit of internet research he would learn the truth regardless. "He was murdered."

Silently, Mac waited.

She took a deep breath, forcing herself to continue. "My name wasn't always Emily Gilley."

"I see that." Tapping the copies of the adoption papers he'd been handed, he eyed her with a law enforcement officer's intent stare. She'd become very familiar with that look in the months immediately following her husband's death.

Steeling herself, she continued trying to relive a past she'd hated. "After the investigation, I learned some things—a lot of things—that I hadn't known about my husband."

"Go on."

"My husband was Carlos Cavell. I had my name legally changed to Gilley after his death." She did this right before she and Ryan had vanished from their old life.

Immediate comprehension dawned in Mac's face. After all, everyone knew of Carlos Cavell. The name had been blazed everywhere in the news after his particularly gruesome murder. Though she'd tried to stay out of the spotlight, inevitably photos of her and Ryan had appeared. Since then, she'd changed her appearance quite a bit. So far, that had been enough.

"Not a bad disguise," Mac commented wryly. "But you still haven't told me why you felt the need to disappear."

"Whoever killed Carlos—and the police were unable to determine even a reasonable suspect—came after me and my son."

Agitated, unable to sit still, she began pacing. "I think it might have been one of his mistresses. I told the police that and they investigated, but they couldn't find anything. So I did the only thing I could. I sold everything, took whatever cash was left after paying the debts and ran."

"Here, to Anniversary."

"Yes. Until now, we were settling in nicely. I really liked it here."

Mac immediately picked up on her use of past tense. "Liked? Are you planning on leaving?"

Chewing on her thumbnail, she forced herself to stop. "I'm not sure. If this keeps up, I have no choice."

"You don't even know if this incident is related."

"How can it not be?" Emily protested. "This intruder took Ryan's adoption records. That was the crux of the threats to begin with. Something about the way Carlos got our son."

"Did he use an adoption service?"

"No. It was a private adoption. Apparently lots of money changed hands. I'm guessing, though I don't know for sure, that whatever channels Carlos went through weren't exactly on the up-and-up."

"As long as both parties signed the necessary paperwork and the documents were filed in a court of law…"

With her throat closing up from the panicked feeling in her chest, she debated whether to go on. In the end, she couldn't risk Mac not understanding the awful truth she suspected—that Ryan was her husband's natural son with one of his mistresses. No way was she letting anyone take her son away from her. She'd die first.

In a quiet voice, she relayed her suspicions.

"I've tried to trace the adoption," she admitted. "Any records beyond what I had were completely destroyed. It's possible—though not certain—that my husband may have obtained Ryan's birth certificate illegally."

To his credit, Mac showed no reaction—as if he heard stories like this every day. Then again, maybe he did.

"So what you're telling me is that you aren't one hundred percent sure you have a legal right to your boy."

Just hearing the words made Emily feel as though she'd been punched in the stomach. She wanted to double over, and only a supreme act of willpower kept her standing upright.

"I—" briefly she closed her eyes "—I don't know."

Now Mac pushed back his chair and stood. As he moved closer, she figured he meant to shake hands and held hers out accordingly.

Instead, to her complete and utter shock, he wrapped his muscular arms around her and gave her a quick hug.

"I'll keep this information between us for the time being. Right now, our focus is on finding whoever wrote you that letter and broke into your house."

Blinking back tears, she stepped out of his embrace and nodded. "Thank you."

Expression enigmatic, he simply watched her, as though waiting for her to say something else.

Chapter 4

Not reacting as Emily bared her soul to him was one of the most difficult things Mac had ever done. Only years of training and working on the streets enabled him to keep his face expressionless. When he'd impulsively hugged her, he half expected her to shove him away and order him to leave.

Instead, she finally nodded and thanked him. He felt thankful that she had no idea of the emotions swirling inside him. He couldn't stop marveling, amazed and humbled by the way he felt now that he'd finally gotten to see his son—after five years, three months and twenty days of missing him and wondering what had happened to him.

One look and he'd known. Even though he hadn't yet taken the DNA test, he knew Ryan was his. Gazing at the dark-headed boy, he saw his wife, Sarah, in the boy's chin, the tilt of his head. And Ryan had Mac's eyes and nose and the full head of dark hair, exactly as Mac had when he'd been a child.

Maybe soon he could reclaim what he'd lost, and they could be a family together.

Then he glanced at Emily, painfully aware of the way she and Ryan interacted. She clearly loved the child she considered her son, and the feeling was mutual. For the first time, Mac wondered what kind of damage he would cause if he tried to take Ryan away from the woman he called Mommy.

Emily cleared her throat, bringing him out of his tangled thoughts. "Well, then. What's your plan?" One brow raised, she waited, a study in contrasts. Her delicately carved facial structure seemed at odds with her lush, passionate mouth. Her short, spiky haircut didn't go with her faded jeans and high-collared blouse.

Eyeing her with as much professional dispassion as he could muster, he cleared his throat. "I have a few more questions about your life before you moved here."

"I see." Appearing resolute, she indicated the kitchen table. Graceful and willowy, her exquisite beauty made her appear both fragile and wild. "Go ahead."

"I need to know…" He paused, searching for the right words. The question he wanted to ask her was one he'd wondered ever since he'd learned she'd adopted the infant he believed was his son. "I need to know if you knew there was something unusual about where your son came from."

Was that guilt that flashed across her mobile face or sorrow?

"No," she said.

He decided to continue to press her. "You never questioned your husband?"

"I never had a reason to, before all this started." Her

careful, measured movements spoke of the depths of her agitation. "You have to understand that being married to a man like Carlos Cavell came with some benefits. One of these seemed to be the ability to cut through a lot of red tape. When we originally applied to adopt an infant, we were told it could take up to three years."

Keeping his expression neutral, he nodded. "And how long in actuality before you were told about Ryan?"

"Six months." She looked down, as though her answer was somehow shameful. And maybe it was, he thought, because any sensible, rational woman should have suspected something was wrong. Or would they?

"Did you go through the same agency that you initially applied to?"

Lifting one shoulder in a shrug, she still wouldn't meet his gaze. "Honestly, at the time, I didn't even question anything. I was just so overjoyed to be getting a baby of my own."

Waiting, he eyed her while she took a deep breath, then looked down. "Actually, I've been unable to make any of the records he had in Ryan's file match up with anything even remotely concrete."

Squinting at her, watching for even the slightest sign that she was hiding something, he waited. He'd long ago learned in situations like this that silence seemed to generate more answers than questions.

Finally, after appearing to be lost in thought, she raised her head and again met his gaze, her big brown eyes soft and defenseless and absolutely beautiful. He felt an unwilling jolt of attraction, which he quickly suppressed.

"You must have your own thoughts about that," he said, his even tone belying the importance of the question. "Where do you think Carlos got Ryan?" His heart pounded as he waited to hear what she would say.

"As I mentioned, my, er, husband had a mistress. Actually, more than one." She gave him a stiff smile, unable to disguise her worry and her hurt. "I'm thinking that Ryan is actually Carlos's son with one of them. He must have forced her into signing the adoption papers. Now she wants her son back. Honestly, if that was the case, I can't help but feel sorry for her."

Startled, he managed to keep his expression noncommittal. "That's one possibility," he said, though in truth he knew it wasn't. "We'll definitely check into that."

She nodded. "Look, Mac—I mean, Deputy Riordan. I don't understand any of this." Though she squared her shoulders and lifted her chin, the quiver in her voice, whether genuine or artificial, made him want to comfort her. No doubt, he thought cynically, that was what she'd hoped for.

Chiding himself silently, he tried to remember he wanted to keep an open mind. There was a chance, no matter how small, that she might not have known that her baby had been stolen right out of the hospital nursery. Emily Gilley could be, as unlikely as it might seem, entirely blameless.

Plus, there was one other thing he needed to consider. When Renee Beauchamp had sworn him in as a deputy, he'd taken an oath to protect and serve. No matter what crimes he suspected Emily Gilley of committing, he now had a sworn duty to help her with her current situation, which, he admitted to himself fiercely, he would have regardless. Because anyone threatening her also threatened Ryan.

He needed to get to know her, try to figure out what

kind of person she was and if she could have knowingly taken someone else's child and claimed him as her own.

Someone else's child. He gave himself a mental shake. It was time to stop hiding from the painful truth.

If what he suspected was factual and Emily Gilley had stolen his son from the hospital nursery, then Ryan Gilley was actually *his* son, the only family he had left in the world.

Mac could only hope this was true. Otherwise, he had no lead to go on, no chance in hell of finding his boy.

While he'd searched for his missing child for five years now without success, he'd begun to despair of ever actually finding him—especially as time went on.

This, too, was his fault. He couldn't help but blame himself. If he'd been more vigilant, he would have managed to keep his son safe. But everything had happened so damn fast. The car crash that had killed his wife, Sarah, had consumed him, and he'd barely acknowledged the baby they'd been able to save. Occupied with an awful grief, he'd buried Sarah, meanwhile trying to figure out how on earth he was going to manage a tiny infant. The day after the funeral, the hospital had called him with the news.

His baby had gone missing right out of the nursery. His department, his own coworkers—people he'd worked with side by side, day in and day out—had handled the case for him since he'd been banned from working on it.

As if that had stopped him. But when lead after lead hadn't panned out and years had gone by, he'd gradually begun to lose hope until his partner, Joe, had uncovered information leading to Emily Gilley and her adopted son, Ryan. Everything—from the adoption shrouded in secrecy, to the time frame and age of her child—pointed to her.

All he needed was proof. And truthfully, he also wanted to know why. He couldn't imagine what kind of twisted, desperate need would drive someone to steal another's child.

Looking at Emily Gilley with an instinct he'd honed after years of police work, he wouldn't have thought she'd be capable of such a heinous act—her husband, maybe, but not her.

The need for answers had been gnawing inside him for months now. If he could prove without a doubt that her son, Ryan, was actually his boy, the infant he and Sarah had decided to call Taylor, Mac intended to get him back in his life—no matter what.

The longer she sat across from Mac Riordan in her brightly painted kitchen, the more uncomfortable Emily became. This room, with its deep red walls and clean white cabinets, had been the only one she'd bothered to change in the rental house. She'd made the kitchen into her sanctuary, envisioning casual meals and noisy children's birthday parties and early morning cups of coffee while the sun rose.

Now, with the big man wearing the deputy sheriff's badge pinned on his impossibly broad chest sitting across from her, the kitchen suddenly seemed too small, closed in, almost alien. She felt as if she were actually seated in a police interrogation room, being questioned about some crime that she hadn't committed.

Ridiculous. Her imagination, always exaggerated, wasn't doing her any favors here. After all, *she had done nothing wrong*.

But a certain cynical look in Mac's bright blue eyes

made her feel culpable somehow, which again, was absurd. She was the victim here, not the perpetrator.

She didn't know the man, so how could she even think she could decipher any expression in his vivid gaze?

While he appeared lost in thought, she studied him. His prematurely gray hair, rather than aging him, gave his craggy face character. Just one look from his sapphire eyes brought a visceral shock that she felt deep within her belly.

He unsettled her. It was strange and disconcerting, too, to say the least. These feelings were entirely unwelcome. She had no business being attracted to a man—any man—when her life was entirely in turmoil.

"All right," he finally said, appearing to reach some sort of decision. "Let's talk about suspects. We've got potential mistresses. Earlier, you mentioned some guy you went on a blind date with. Tell me about him."

She sighed, thinking of her failed attempt to be normal. "I'm pretty sure Tim is harmless."

"Let me be the judge of that."

Instead of fixating on the way his mouth quirked appealingly at the corner, she swallowed. "Would you like something to drink?" she asked, because she needed a distraction. "I've got iced tea, lemonade and water."

"Water would be great."

Glad she was able to occupy herself by filling two glasses with ice, then the cold water she kept in a pitcher in the fridge, she turned and placed their drinks on the kitchen table.

He reached for the glass. "Thank you," he said, drinking deeply. She found herself watching the strong lines of his throat as he drank. "About this Tim. What's his last name?"

"Keeslar. Tim Keeslar. My friend Tina set this up. You've met her. She's a waitress at Sue's Catfish Hut."

He nodded, writing down the last name. "Tell me everything you know about him."

"I really don't think—"

"Please." He touched the back of her hand, his fingers both protective and soothing. "Humor me."

"He's tall and slender, longish dark hair. Not bad looking." She shrugged, slightly embarrassed. "He owns his own home and drives a big Ford pickup."

"What does he do for a living?"

"He owns the auto-parts store on Fifth Street."

After noting all this, Mac looked up, brow raised. "And he's single? Has he ever been married?"

"I don't think so, but I can't say for sure. We only went out twice." She rubbed her suddenly aching temples, trying to remember. "I don't know."

"That's okay. I can easily find that out. Tell me why you thought he might be your stalker. You said he liked you way more than you liked him."

Feeling foolish, she relayed how, after declining a third date, Tim suddenly started popping up everywhere she went. "If I went to a movie with Jayne or Tina, Tim was there. I couldn't go anywhere—the grocery store, the dry cleaners, downtown—without running into him."

"Did you confront him?"

She gave him a wry smile. "I'm pretty sure you know the answer to that."

He asked a few more questions. He was very thorough, and she liked the way he carefully noted her responses.

"*Now* do you take me seriously?" Emily asked him

quietly, amazed at her sense of relief now that she'd gotten everything off her shoulders.

He gave her a sharp look and a frown. "Emily, I've always taken you seriously. I'd be a fool to do anything else."

Then, while she was puzzling over his cryptic statement, he drained the last of his water, stood and dipped his chin. "I'll be in touch," he said, and let himself out.

Driving back to his fledgling trucking company, Mac mulled over the dramatic change that had occurred in his life—almost overnight. Originally, he'd come to Anniversary with no plans to ever work again in law enforcement.

Using his savings, he'd started up a trucking company, specializing in flatbed freight hauling. To his surprise, business had been good—so good, in fact, that earlier that week he'd decided he needed to hire his first nondriver employee. He needed someone to book loads both through trucking brokers and directly through shippers using not only the phone but personal contacts and the internet. This meant he had to find someone with trucking experience who didn't want to be a truck driver.

This was not a small order in a town the size of Anniversary.

He had an interview scheduled that afternoon with the first person to respond to his ad, a young man named Chris Pitts. According to the résumé he'd emailed, his father and two brothers were all truckers, which of course made Mac wonder why Chris wasn't.

He had an immediate answer to that question when Chris rolled into his shop in a wheelchair.

"Old football injury," he said in response to Mac's

questioning look. "Can't climb in and out of a truck. Also, my body can't take the pounding of the road. But I can still work, just not as a truck driver."

"As long as you keep my trucks loaded, you can do laps around the yard in your wheelchair if you want," Mac responded. When Chris grinned, Mac knew that, barring any real oddities in the interview, he'd found his dispatcher.

Even better, Chris wanted to start work immediately. "Tomorrow morning?"

"I'll be here." The two men shook hands, and Chris wheeled himself out. Following, Mac watched as the younger man used a specially equipped van. He stepped forward, but Chris waved off his offer of assistance.

"I've got it. I've been doing this on my own for a few years now." Chris flashed another big grin, and after stowing his wheelchair via an electronic lift, waved and drove away.

Watching him go, for the first time in far too long, Mac thought his life might finally be on the right track. He was once again doing the kind of work he'd been born to do and—even better—his job gave him up close and personal access to not only Emily Gilley but Ryan. He couldn't have planned things better if he'd tried.

After Mac left, Emily tried to put her house back in some semblance of order. At odd intervals, tears threatened, which infuriated her as she angrily wiped them away. How long would she and Ryan have to pay for a greedy, unethical man's misdeeds? She'd been naive and foolish when she'd married Carlos Cavell, looking past the gaping inconsistencies between what he told her and the reality of his actual life.

In fact, she'd been so willingly blinded that it wasn't

until after Carlos's death that she'd learned not only had he kept more than one longtime mistress but he'd been involved in some shady if not outright illegal deals and left her in debt up to her eyeballs.

The chain of restaurants that she'd believed provided their income were barely functional, losing money and, if the NYPD were to be believed, operated as a front for Carlos's money-laundering operations. There'd been debts and deals and a stack of unpaid bills.

She'd been in the process of selling everything, including her lavish home, when the first threat had arrived. To her horror and shock, the double-paged rambling missive had hinted that she'd somehow stolen her son. This had so terrified her that she'd rushed to check the adoption records even before contacting the authorities.

All the paperwork on Ryan's adoption appeared to be in order, but appearances were deceiving. After making a few phone calls and doing some online research, she learned the adoption broker listed had never existed.

In other words, the adoption papers were entirely fake—forged by Carlos or his associates. For what reason, she had no idea.

Truth be told, she really didn't want to know. Ryan had come to her an infant and, at the time of Carlos's death, was still a tiny human being who was her son— body, heart and spirit. They were linked in deeper ways than mere flesh and blood.

She couldn't take a chance losing him.

So she'd kept silent about the threats, continued liquidating her assets, paying off the debts and making plans.

Then when she had nothing left to tie her to Manhattan, she and Ryan had gotten up one morning and quietly disappeared.

Now that four and a half uneventful years had passed since she'd left, she'd begun to relax, to allow herself to feel safe.

Not anymore, though. It appeared her stalker had finally found her.

By the time the sun began to rise, Emily had nearly finished downing her second cup of strong coffee. She sat alone in the kitchen, one scented candle her only source of light. Ryan still slept, blissfully unaware of the storm clouds of chaos threatening his world.

What to do, what to do... Every instinct screamed *run,* but truth be told, she was tired of running. She'd settled in here in Anniversary, loving the feeling of actually living an ordinary life.

Still, she had to face facts. If she didn't run, then what were her options? If she stayed and fought, she'd have to learn who the stalker was and what exactly he or she wanted.

Most importantly, was Ryan at risk? Restless, she got up and poured herself another cup.

First there was the cryptic note, then the break-in. What next?

Picking up the note, she reread the words. *I know what you've done. You've stolen what is mine, and you'll pay for what you did. Tell the truth or risk everything.*

Hand shaking, she read it again. It was cryptic, to be sure. But she had nothing of value except her child.

While she knew she didn't know what really had happened with her son's adoption, she'd done nothing more than welcome an infant into her life five years ago. Believing her husband was on the up-and-up, she'd been full of happiness to finally have the child she was unable to conceive—Ryan…her boy…her son.

Since then, she'd given him everything a child could want, not the least of all which was her heart. As to telling the truth, how could she do that when she didn't even know what it was?

Forcing herself to be analytical, she read the note a third time. All of the messages had been variations of this same threat. She'd stolen something from the stalker. Tell the truth or risk everything. Renee was right. As far as threats went, that was awfully vague. She supposed she ought to be grateful the stalker hadn't written something like "you and the boy will die."

But despite the lack of specification, the notes still terrified her. She supposed she really didn't want to know the truth, didn't want to learn what her husband had done to bring her this child.

Because, in the end, none of it mattered. Ryan was hers. She'd give her life protecting him if it came to that.

Pacing, steaming cup of coffee in hand, Emily eyed the clock, willing her heartbeat to slow. She couldn't think rationally if she allowed panic to take over.

First things first, she had to decide what course of action, if any, to take immediately. As the first light of sunrise began to dapple the trees, she took a deep breath. She decided to call in to work and ask for the day off. Once she let them know what had happened, she felt certain they'd be sympathetic, which was just one of the reasons she loved working there.

Aware the clinic opened at seven for surgery drop-offs, she made the call and, exactly as she'd suspected, she was told in no uncertain terms to take a personal day.

Hanging up the phone, she poured another cup of

coffee. As she did, the tightness in her chest eased somewhat. Funny how accomplishing even one small thing made her feel a tiny bit better, more in control of her life.

Next, she debated whether or not to take Ryan to school. In the end, she decided normalcy would be the best for him, so she woke him and helped him choose his clothes for the day.

Driving him to kindergarten, the sheer ordinariness of the act made her regret taking the entire day off from work. But after seeing her son safely ensconced in his classroom under the watchful eye of Ms. Penney, she headed home to try and make order of her ransacked home.

As soon as she got there, though, she decided to go in to work for the afternoon, once she'd finished straightening out her house.

An hour or so later, having tidied the living room and gotten her office back into some semblance of order, she wandered into the kitchen to see if she could squeeze one final cup of coffee from the nearly empty pot. As she sipped the lukewarm beverage, she eyed the clock. If she made herself a quick lunch and changed clothes, she could arrive at the office shortly after noon.

Later, after arriving at the bustling veterinary clinic, she was glad she'd decided to go in. The busy ordinary workday would help take her mind off her problems. She needed to be calm and rational in order to think.

Luckily, the day flew by. A steady stream of clients kept her busy. Before she knew it, the wall clock showed five minutes until closing time.

Just as she was about to lock up and head out, her cell phone rang. It was Mrs. Mims, the day care director and owner.

"Emily, you'd better get over here quick," she said, her normally calm voice quivering.

Instantly, Emily's heart leapt into her throat. She asked about Ryan. "Is he all right?"

"He's fine," Mrs. Mims assured her, clearly trying for calm, although she sounded out of breath and agitated. "But earlier—" she hesitated, then continued in a rush "—a man tried to grab him off the playground. His teacher and one of the parents were able to stop him. The sheriff's department is on the way."

Chapter 5

Heart pounding, Emily murmured something in reply and hung up the phone. After she grabbed her purse, she rushed to the front door, dizzy and nauseated. Someone had tried to snatch Ryan. The words played over and over again, a terrifying litany echoing inside her head.

Had this been completely random, the act of some sick pervert wanting a child, any child? Or was this tied into the threats and her past life? Did they even matter? Either way, her son had nearly been harmed.

Taking deep breaths and fighting off the dizziness and the panic, she broke every speed limit on the way to the day care. When she pulled up, two police cars blocked the entrance, lights flashing blue, white and red.

Once she'd parked behind them, she cut the engine and ran to the entrance. Renee Beauchamp and Mac

Riordan waited just inside the doorway, with a clearly rattled Mrs. Mims.

Emily hurried forward, and Mac moved to intercept her.

"Easy now," he said, correctly interpreting Emily's frantic fears. "Everything's going to be all right." He spoke in a soothing voice, taking Emily's arm and steering her into Mrs. Mims's office. "Ryan's fine."

A single chair rested in front of Mrs. Mims's desk. Emily had sat there once before, when she'd enrolled her son in the day care, and later the after-school program. As she let Mac guide her to that seat now, she realized her entire body had begun to tremble.

"I want to see my son." She forced out the words through lifeless lips. "Please."

Before she'd even finished speaking, Renee shepherded Ryan into the office. Emily shot up out of the chair, dropping to her knees and enveloping her boy into a tight hug.

"Mommy?" Squirming, Ryan pushed her away. "What's wrong?"

It dawned on her that her son had no idea of the danger he'd just faced. Emily took a deep breath. When she looked up and met Mac's gaze, she realized he looked nearly as rattled as she felt.

"Nothing's the matter," she managed, swallowing hard. "I just missed you."

Nodding, Ryan appeared to accept this at face value. Then, with a five-year-old's aplomb, he eyed Renee and Mac, his expression grave. "Was there an accident?"

Exchanging a quick look with Emily, Mac squatted down to put himself at Ryan's level. "No, not exactly. We wanted to talk to you about the man you met earlier, when you were in the playground."

Ryan's troubled expression cleared. "Oh, him. He wasn't a bad man."

Emily's heart skipped a beat, but she managed to keep her expression neutral. "How do you know he wasn't bad, honey?"

"Because even though he was just like that man in that movie—you know—*Stranger Danger,* he really didn't want to hurt me."

Mac crouched down, putting himself at Ryan's level. "Why don't you tell us exactly what happened?"

"Okay." Moving in closer to Emily, as though he needed reassurance, Ryan appeared to carefully consider his words, adopting a serious manner far older than his five years. "First, he said he had candy, and if I wanted to have some I had to go with him."

Emily winced. Feeling the sudden tension in his mother's body, Ryan stopped, peering up at her. "Mommy? Are you all right?"

Only when she'd nodded and tried to smile reassuringly did he continue. "When I told him no, he said he had puppies in his van. Just like the cartoon we watched in preschool," Ryan said scornfully. "I'm only five, and I know better than that."

"Van?" Mac asked, his deliberately casual voice at odds with his intense gaze. "What color was the van?"

Ryan shrugged. "I don't know. I never saw it. He said it was parked around the corner." Then, again looking up at his mother, he scrunched up his little freckled face into a concerned frown. "You told me never to go with strangers, right Mommy?"

Chest so tight she wasn't certain she could speak, Emily nodded. "Yes, I did, Ryan." Praying her hand wouldn't shake too badly, she reached out and ruffled his hair. "You did good, son. I'm proud of you."

Ruffling Ryan's hair, Mac stood. "Let me take you home," Mac murmured to Emily.

"I don't want to go home," she said, surprising even herself. Then, noting the way Ryan gazed up at her in concern, she forced another smile. "I was thinking about taking Ryan out for pizza since he did so well today."

Ryan beamed. Looking from his mother to Mac, he smiled. "You can come, too, Mac," he offered. "Mommy might feel better if we have a policeman with us."

Raising a brow, Mac and her son shared a conspiratorial grin. "Pizza it is," he said, as though he knew there was no way Emily would refuse him.

And he was right, she thought ruefully as she walked, still weak-kneed, toward the door with her son and the man who'd promised to protect them.

When Mac held out his hand for Emily's keys, he half expected her to ignore him. It was a testament to her state of mind when she simply handed them over without a word.

Driving with Emily in the passenger seat and Ryan buckled into his booster seat in the back, he couldn't help but imagine if this is what it would be like to be a family—something he'd always wanted and knew he'd never have.

From the pinched look on Emily's face and Ryan's uncharacteristic silence, he doubted either of them was thinking along the same lines.

"Are you all right, little buddy?" he asked, watching the boy who might be his son in the rearview mirror.

Ryan nodded without speaking. Mac glanced at Emily, half expecting her to crumple at any moment and dissolve in tears, which wouldn't be good—at all. He needed her to be able to stay strong to protect her son.

Instead, she sat ramrod straight, staring ahead and lost in thought. Judging from the set of her jaw, she was furious.

Good. That meant she wouldn't give up without a fight. He reluctantly admired that.

They arrived at Paul's Pizza Palace, which he was pleased to note wasn't overly crowded. He parked the car and hurried to open Emily's door, then stood guard while she helped Ryan out of his booster seat.

Once inside, they went through the buffet line and, plates stacked high, they followed while Emily chose a booth. Mac approved of her choice. Away from the windows and tucked into a back corner with a good view of the door, they had both privacy and a clear escape route if needed.

Chiding himself for being paranoid, he ate his pizza and tried to relax. This should be a moment he savored. It wasn't every day he got to share a meal with the boy who might be his son.

He'd nearly succeeded when Emily touched his arm. "I know that man."

At the urgency in her voice, Mac turned to see who she meant. Across the room crowded with lunchtime diners, his new dispatcher Chris sat with his chair wheeled up to a table.

Eyes wide and stricken, Emily had gone pale as a sheet. "What's he doing here?" she whispered.

"That's my dispatcher, Chris," Mac said. He tried to sound normal despite the fact that she looked like she'd seen a demon emerge from the bowels of hell. "Do you know him?"

"Yes." Mouth grim, she nodded. "His name isn't really Chris."

Silently, Mac cursed. He should have run a comprehensive background check. "Are you sure?"

"Yes." Studiously avoiding glancing across the room, Emily pretended to study the menu. "That's Franco DiSorinne. He was one of my husband's most trusted men."

Mac clenched his jaw, resisting the urge to reach across the table and take her hand in his. "Okay, say it is him. Do you have any idea why he would be here, pretending to be someone else? It's been what, five years since Carlos died?"

When she raised her head to meet his gaze, he saw panic in her eyes. "I don't know. I've received various threats over the years, but until recently, they'd died out." Shaking, she leaned close so Ryan wouldn't hear. "We need to find out if he's the man who tried to grab Ryan."

Glancing at Ryan, who had finished his pizza and was busy playing a game on Emily's phone, Mac shook his head. "He didn't say anything about a wheelchair," he said, sotto voce.

"Wheelchairs can be fake," she shot back in a whisper. "You should know that better than anyone. I'll bet he can walk just fine. Franco wasn't in a wheelchair the last time I saw him."

Debating whether to confront his dispatcher here or wait until Chris—er, Franco—showed up for work in the morning, Mac decided there was no better time than the present.

He pushed up from the booth and stood. But when he glanced across the room, Chris was gone.

"I'll talk to him in the morning," he said, meeting

Emily's troubled gaze and holding it. Unable to help himself, he reached across the table and covered her hand with his own. "Don't worry. If he's behind this, we'll take care of it."

Though she nodded, the worry and fear never left her eyes. "You know what?" she announced, pushing her barely touched meal away. "I'd prefer if you could clear this up tonight. Right now, I'd like to go home and let you get out there and do your job."

Since he couldn't fault her logic, he nodded. Ryan had finished eating and bounced in his seat, asking to go to the video arcade every few minutes. Undeterred by his mother's constant *no*'s, he continued to push, sending Emily perilously close to the edge.

When Mac stood, a clearly relieved Emily helped Ryan to his feet. "We're going home," she said firmly, steering him away from the brightly lit arcade.

"I'll need you to drop me off at the day care so I can pick up my car," Mac said quietly. Emily nodded, and again he felt the urge to comfort her, to reach across the seat and pull her into his side. Of course, he did nothing.

They drove away in silence, both lost in their own thoughts, managing to ignore Ryan's persistent, low-key whining.

When they pulled up in front of the day care, Renee's department vehicle was still parked in the lot. Mac got out, taking one final long look at Ryan, so he could sear the image on his heart. He told a clearly distracted Emily goodbye, advising her to make sure she locked all her doors, and watched as she drove off.

Then he climbed into his police cruiser and went looking for Chris Pitts, aka Franco DiSorinne.

An hour and a half later, he admitted defeat. Nothing checked out—not the information Chris had put on his employment application or a search of the state database. Neither Chris Pitts or Franco DiSorinne were listed as residents of Texas.

Weary, he decided to call it a night. On his way home, he ran through a drive-thru and picked up a burger and fries for dinner. It was not the healthiest solution, he knew, but with the kind of day he'd had, the last thing he felt like doing was cooking anything.

Once home, he walked out to the small wooden building he used as his trucking company office. Even though Chris or Franco had only worked as his dispatcher for a short time, he'd done a wonderful job. Not only would he be sorely missed but next to impossible to replace. Every truck had remained loaded and busy, and Chris had even set up some bookings for the rest of the week.

Mac grimaced. It was too bad he'd somehow found the perfect employee who'd turned out to be bogus.

Returning to his kitchen, he sighed and opened the takeout bag and began to chow down, standing up. As he finished eating, washing down his food with a cold beer, his cell phone rang. Caller ID showed it was his friend and former partner, Joe Stalling.

"Hey, Joe." Grinning, Mac took a swig of his beer and leaned back in his chair. Since Joe still worked as a detective for the Albany P.D., his calls always filled Mac in on all the happenings there.

"Hey, yourself." Joe's grin came across in his voice. That was one of the things Mac had liked best about the other man—his tendency to find amusement in the worst situations. Considering his job, working in the Crimes Against Persons—Family Unit, and the types of gut-wrenching cases he'd had, Joe was lucky to have managed to avoid burnout after five years at the same job.

Others sometimes found his ever-present smile off-putting. But Mac knew each officer had his own way of dealing with all the horrific and senseless acts of violence. Joe's dogged sense of humor was his.

Mac trusted him more than he had anyone since his wife Sarah. They'd all been good friends, back in the days before the car accident had taken Sarah's life. In fact, Joe was the only person who knew the true reason Mac had resigned from the force and moved to Texas. He filled Joe in on taking the part-time job with the local police department but made no mention of Emily or her break-in.

"Have you seen the kid yet?" Joe asked.

Mac hesitated. He didn't know why, but he didn't want to admit that he'd met Ryan. For now, he wanted to keep it private, between him and Emily and the boy.

"No," he lied. "I've only just met Emily, the mother. I'm trying to take things slow."

The other man snorted. "Hell, you've been there over three weeks. How much slower can you go?"

Taking another swig of beer, Mac decided not to respond. Instead, he cut directly to the chase. "Do you have any new info for me about Cavell or his wife?" Joe had promised to use the vast law enforcement network to keep Mac informed if anything else surfaced about Emily's former husband.

"There's a ton of information, but I had to jump through hoops to get it." Joe sighed. "Since I'm in Albany, upstate, it hasn't been easy. NYPD is pretty tight about releasing anything to an outside agency."

Startled, Mac blinked. "NYPD? This was a federal investigation. Since you worked with them once, I thought you were going through them."

"I'm trying, but you know as well as I do that getting anything from the Feds is like pulling teeth. I'm also relying on an old friend at the NYPD. He's worked there for years."

Mac frowned. This didn't make a lot of sense. While agencies frequently shared information, the Feds were notoriously tight-lipped with cases of this caliber, which was no doubt still going on since Carlos Cavell's death was the only part of the huge investigation that had actually been solved. They'd have been more likely to talk directly to Joe since he'd done work with them in the past on this case. Mac didn't think they would share with NYPD unless they had a damn good reason.

However, Joe had no reason to lie. If he said NYPD had info, then Mac believed him.

"So did you get something?" Mac asked.

"Yep, though I don't know if there's anything useful. My contact emailed me everything he had. There's a lot of paper. I'm sorting through it bit by bit. I'm hoping to finish up by the end of this week."

"Thanks." Curious, Mac scratched his head. "What reason did you give NYPD for wanting copies of the files?"

Joe laughed. "First off, I didn't go through official channels. Second, I used the good old standard— ongoing investigation. My buddy didn't ask a lot of questions. He owed me a favor, so I called it in."

"I really appreciate that," Mac said and meant it.

"No problem. Hey, Mac?" Joe's voice rang with fierce determination. "When you get to see the kid, take a cell phone picture or something and send it to me. I'd really like to see it, okay?"

Mac found himself grinning, his inner turmoil easing somewhat. Sometimes he really missed his friend. "Sure will, buddy. Talk to you later."

Placing the phone on the table, Mac picked at the last of his fries. Joe was so hopeful for him and really enthusiastic over the prospect of Mac finally being reunited with his son. Mac appreciated that. It felt good to actually have a good friend on his side—especially since Joe's tireless efforts on Mac's behalf had led to him being the one to actually find Ryan.

Scratching his head, he drained his beer. He couldn't help but wonder why he felt so reluctant to share his good fortune with Joe. Maybe it was because he didn't yet know the truth. That had to be it.

Satisfied, he wandered into the living room and turned on the TV. For the first time in years, he found himself looking forward to tomorrow and the new day. Maybe in Anniversary he'd finally found a place he could call home.

When the doorbell chimed a little after 5:00 p.m., Emily's first inclination was to ignore it. After all, she and Ryan were going to spend the next couple of hours lounging in front of the TV, trying to regain a sense of normalcy.

Still, just in case Mac had decided to come back for some reason, she looked through the peephole.

An unfamiliar blonde woman stood on her front step. She was young, pretty, and wearing a low-cut, formfitting red dress and four-inch platform heels that wouldn't have been out of place on a stripper. Curious, Emily opened the door. "Yes?"

Long-lashed and heavily made-up brown eyes stared her down. "Are you Emily Cavell?"

Instantly, silent alarms went off. "My last name is Gilley," Emily answered. "What do you want?"

Undeterred by Emily's icy tone, the blonde continued to study her. "I'm Desiree. Maybe Carlos mentioned me?"

Carlos. With dawning horror, Emily realized who this woman was. She was one of Carlos's former mistresses. Her heart began to pound. It took every ounce of willpower not to slam the door in the woman's face.

"What do you want?" Emily asked again.

"I need to talk to you." Desiree looked pointedly past Emily toward the living room. "Can I come in?"

"No." No way was she letting this woman inside the house where her son lay sleeping. Instead, she stepped outside, closing the door firmly behind her. "If you want to talk, then talk," she ordered. "Otherwise, I'm going to have to ask you to leave."

"Oh, not yet," Desiree said grimly. "Not until I've gotten what I came for."

At that moment, Emily realized the vulnerable position she'd just put herself in. Unarmed, without even her cell phone, she stood outside in plain view. If anyone wanted to ambush her, she'd be easy pickings.

Instead of responding to what sounded like an overt threat, Emily simply crossed her arms and waited. She kept her back to the door, the handle within reach in case she needed to beat a hasty retreat.

"Carlos gave me some jewelry," Desiree said when it became apparent that Emily wasn't going to question her. "A beautiful diamond necklace and tennis bracelet. He took them to get them professionally cleaned."

"And?"

Desiree coughed delicately. "Well, he died before returning them. I'd like to get them back."

Though her relief was so great that Emily nearly laughed out loud, she managed to keep her face expressionless. She'd thought this woman had come looking for her son. Instead, she wanted some baubles?

"Was that what this was all about? The threats, the break-in?"

"Threats? Break-in?" Desiree sounded genuinely puzzled. "I have no idea what you're talking about. A friend in the NYPD told me I would get my jewelry back when the investigation into Carlos's death was complete. But I didn't."

"The investigation wound down several years ago," Emily pointed out.

"I know." Desiree pouted prettily. "And believe me, I was bummed when you disappeared. But my friend found you and told me to go see you. So here I am. I'm ready to collect what belongs to me."

Emily froze. The last sentence was lifted right out of the threatening notes. Suddenly afraid, she forced herself to lift her chin and hide her fear. "I'm sorry. I don't have your jewelry."

Desiree frowned, a small crease forming between her perfectly shaped brows. "I don't believe you."

"Everything Carlos had was liquidated to pay debts. I never saw any diamond necklace or bracelet."

"These were very valuable—" Desiree began.

Emily had had enough. "I understand, and I'm sorry," she said, turning to go back inside.

Desiree grabbed her arm. "I've come a long way. I'll report you for theft."

Emily jerked away, heart beating a furious tattoo in her chest. "Go right ahead. Now I'm asking you to leave my property."

The other woman didn't move. "Or what?"

"Or I'm calling the police."

Inside, the phone rang. Praying Desiree wouldn't try to force her way inside, Emily turned, yanked open the door, stepped around it and slammed it closed in the other woman's face. Still stunned and shaken, she slid the dead bolt into place before running to grab the still-ringing phone.

"Emily?"

Mac. She closed her eyes. Thank God. "Please come," she croaked. "Come quick."

Five minutes later, she heard his car screech down her street and pull up in her driveway. By the time he reached her front door, she thought she'd managed to pull herself together, gathering her shredded composure into some semblance of rational normalcy.

Yanking open the door, she stepped aside so he could enter. Instead, he pulled her close for a quick hug. Dazedly, she wondered if he hugged all his victims.

Once he'd released her, she swallowed hard and raised her head. "One of Carlos's mistresses was here."

Mac nodded. Jaw clenched and steely eyed, he looked both concerned and furious. "Tell me what happened."

When she relayed what Desiree had said, his expression grew thunderous. "Did she admit to breaking into your house?"

"No." She pushed away the urge to step closer to him in the hopes he'd hold her again. For some foolish reason, being close to him gave her strength.

"What about the threatening note?"

Again she shook her head. "I'm guessing it was her, don't you think?"

"I never guess when it comes to this kind of thing. Remember, we have more than one suspect. There's that guy you dated, Tim Keeslar. I haven't been able to locate him yet. And there's my dispatcher, Chris, or Franco or whatever his name really is. Now we've got this woman."

She watched as he pulled a pad and pen from his pocket. "Tell me everything you remember. What was her name?"

"I almost hate to say it," she admitted. "It's pretty cliché. She said her name was Desiree."

One corner of his mouth twitched, but to his credit, he didn't laugh. He asked several more questions, jotting down all her answers. When he'd finished, he put away the pad and pen and stood staring at her for a moment.

Suddenly tongue-tied, she colored as she realized she'd been staring at his mouth.

Full of longing, she met his gaze, aware he'd most likely been able to see her completely inappropriate desire.

Instead of commenting, he took a step toward her. She moved toward him and somehow wound up exactly where she wanted to be—in his arms.

Chapter 6

He tasted like spearmint and safety, and as Emily relaxed into his embrace, she could feel the tight leash he kept on his passion. Despite that, explosive currents washed over her, making her body throb.

Unconsciously, she leaned into him and deepened the kiss. The sheer maleness of him sent shivers to her core. Briefly, she wondered if he felt the same, then decided she didn't care.

He held her snugly, making no effort to break away, and when she raised her head to take a breath, he reclaimed her lips almost instantly. The kiss was heady, despite its odd gentleness, and left her mouth burning.

She wanted none of this; she wanted more. She wanted…giving up the struggle for rational thought, she returned his kiss with a recklessness that wasn't at all like her.

When they finally broke apart—this time for good—

both of them were breathing heavily. His eyes had gone dark, but his expression had turned to stone.

"That shouldn't have happened," she began. "I—"

"I agree." His harsh voice sounded raw. "Let's pretend it didn't and stick to business."

Though his swift dismissal stung, she knew he was right. While she struggled to organize her thoughts, he moved toward the door. "I'll see what I can find out about this Desiree. If I locate her or find any information about her I'll be in touch."

"Thank you," she answered. "Though I may not be here after today."

He froze. Apparently, that had been the wrong thing to say. "Where will you be?"

With a casual shrug, she hoped her tone sounded as expressionless as his. "I'm thinking about simply packing up and leaving town."

"Running? Again?"

"Don't talk as though you know me," she said, her sharp voice masking her hurt. "I'll do what I think best. I won't leave unless I have to. I want Ryan to have this." She spread her arms, turning to encompass her ordinary house with the lush suburban yard. "A place he can put down roots. Friends he'll have through all his school years. A sense of permanence. I don't want to yank him from town to town, always on the run, always looking over our shoulders."

"That's commendable," he said. "Fighting is always preferable, at least as far as I'm concerned."

There was something in his voice. "Is that what you've done?" she asked softly. "Fought for what you want?"

Her question startled him. Dark emotion flashed in

his eyes a second before he slammed the lid down on it. "It's better than running," he repeated.

She noticed he didn't answer her question. Fine. She didn't really care anyway. She only had enough energy to worry about her son. "If things get bad enough where I have no choice, then both Ryan and I are out of here. We'll go in the night, without notice to you or anyone else. Do you understand?"

"Of course," he said, "but I doubt it's going to come to that. Believe me, I want to catch this guy as bad as you do."

Nodding, she swallowed hard and then took a big leap of faith. "Then I need you to do one more favor for me. I need you to help me find out the truth about Ryan's adoption. I think if I can do that then we can figure out who this crazy person is and why he or she is stalking me."

Despite the earth-shattering honesty of the kiss they'd shared, Mac could barely contain his shock at her trusting words. If Emily truly meant what she'd just said—and the raw sincerity in her voice told him she did—he had to believe she really didn't know what the truth about Ryan.

In all the scenarios he'd imagined, he hadn't thought of this possibility. He'd been prepared for so long to do battle with the woman who'd stolen his son and now... now the best thing he could do was reserve all judgment and guide her to the truth about where her son had come from. But could he do so and remain objective? That was the question. He didn't know the answer, but he'd certainly have to try.

With a start, he realized she watched him with trust and hope shining naked from her beautiful brown eyes.

For half a second he felt like a heel then realized he'd done nothing wrong.

"I know we've been over this, but we need to go over it again. Let's start at the beginning." Hand at the small of her back, he gently guided her toward the house. He liked touching her. Something about her delicate, willowy physique brought out the protector in him. He hadn't felt at all like that in the time since his wife had died and his son disappeared. Since he'd been unable to protect either one of them, he supposed that was natural.

But feeling like that about Emily was all kinds of wrong—at least until they learned the truth about whether or not she and her former husband had been the ones who'd stolen his son.

When she took a seat on her sofa and motioned him to the chair, her caramel eyes blazed with determination and suppressed anger. While he reluctantly admired her spunk, he didn't want her doing anything brave and crazy.

"I've already told you everything I know," she began, her words trailing off as he shook his head.

"I know, but even if we've already gone over this, I want you to tell me everything you remember about adopting Ryan. There might be some kernel of information there that you might have overlooked."

"All right." Sitting back, she briefly closed her eyes, as though she needed to gather her strength to relive the past. Watching her in this unguarded moment, the way the light reflected on her creamy skin and the sexy way the shagginess of her dark hair set off her delicately carved facial structure, he fought the urge to touch her, to pull her close and lend her strength. Ridiculous, yet even as he mentally scoffed at his own foolishness, his body stirred at her unconscious loveliness. She was everything he was not—beauty and grace and compassion, a perfect mother for Ryan. Though her marriage had failed, she'd make some man a wonderful wife.

Damn. Throat aching, he looked away, cursing the fact that he had to struggle to regain his composure. He swallowed hard, and forced himself to concentrate. "Start at the beginning," he urged, his voice remarkably steady. "I assume you and your husband had been trying to conceive."

Her amazing eyes flew open, briefly reflecting her anguish when she thought of that long ago time. For a moment, she bowed her head, and when she lifted it again, he knew how hard it was for her to bare her soul to him.

"Yes," she said. "I wanted children. Carlos said he did, but I think he only agreed because if I was busy with babies he would be free to do whatever he wanted."

Something stirred in him at her unguarded words—something foolish and dangerous and completely misplaced. Clearing his throat, he kept asking the questions that he knew he must. "Yours wasn't a happy marriage?"

"No." The admission seemed to startle her. "I truly didn't know my husband when I married him. I thought I did, really. But like a lot of other young women, I overlooked a lot of things. Many of those I believed I could change once we were married."

"Change how?"

She ducked her head, her face coloring as though embarrassed. "With the power of my love." She sighed, then continued. "I did love him once."

He didn't comment. How could he? Once, he'd been exactly the same with his wife, Sarah. Luckily for them, she'd settled down, tamed her wildness and began working on their marriage. Otherwise, he had no doubt they wouldn't have lasted past the first year.

"I know what you mean. I've forgiven much," he said. "In the name of love."

"Thank you." Her relieved smile told him she appreciated the small kindness. "Anyway, Carlos humored me with what he called the baby obsession. But no matter what, I just couldn't get pregnant."

"So you had tests?"

"No." Her expression clouded. "He refused. I don't think he could have handled it if he learned the infertility was his fault. He was so—" she waved a hand vaguely "—macho, you know?"

He didn't know. He'd never met the man. But from the videos he'd watched of police interrogations, Carlos Cavell had been a preening peacock of a man. Mac couldn't even begin to picture him with a woman like Emily.

"Go on."

Twisting her hands in her lap, she continued. "Anyway, after a while of trying, he said he was done. He told me if I wanted a baby so much, then I needed to go ahead and adopt one. His only stipulation was that the child be a boy."

"He wanted a son." Odd how even now with the other man long dead, the thought could infuriate Mac. Unwilling to wait for the adoption to go through the proper channels, which took time, when Carlos had wanted a son, he'd simply hired someone to steal one.

"Yes. He wanted a son. I would have been happy with either a boy or a girl, so that didn't matter to me."

Briskly, Mac forced himself to continue the questioning. "So you decided to adopt. Who began the process?"

"I did. Carlos was far too busy to have time to do something like that. But when he heard me complaining about how slow everything seemed to be going, he took over."

They covered a few more things, like the fact that every single place she'd contacted had pointed out the long waiting list. Whether church group or private agency, if she wanted an infant, she'd better be prepared to wait.

"And one of the things Carlos didn't have was patience," she said. "He told me he was going to pull some strings. I don't know what he did, but he called me one day and told me to get the nursery ready. Very soon we were going to have our very own baby."

"And you didn't question how he'd accomplished such a miracle in six months' time?"

"We've already covered this." Stretching, she met his gaze, though her own was hooded, looking inward. "I was so overjoyed that I was finally having my dream of a baby come true that I didn't question him. He was my husband."

Mac nodded, wondering why of all the women in the world this one got to him. They should be sworn enemies, and instead, he found himself wanting to hold her. "And then?" he prompted.

"Then, exactly as Carlos had promised, I had my baby. Ryan." Her smile was genuine, full of love. "He was only a few days old when they brought him to me. I've often wondered about the mother who gave him up—even if she was one of Carlos's mistresses, which I've suspected she was."

Carlos's mistresses? Really? It took every ounce of self-control not to react to her comment.

He didn't understand how the hell she could say such a thing. Could she truly believe that Ryan's mother was one of Carlos's many lovers? He truly didn't think Emily was that clueless, but her words left only one possibility—the same one he'd already reached.

She didn't know. He felt it like a physical blow to his chest. She honestly did not know.

Looking down, he briefly closed his eyes. Of all he'd expected when he met this woman and of all the scenarios he'd imagined, he'd never pictured this likelihood.

Emily Gilley might truly be innocent. If she really had no idea at all that the baby she'd adopted had been stolen, then she was blameless, as much of a victim as he was—judging from her statement about Carlos's mistress, She wasn't the slightest bit aware that her son legally belonged to someone else.

Or…he forced himself to hang on to his cynical nature. The other possibility was that Emily was a damn fine actress.

Until he knew for sure, he couldn't allow the lure of her compelling beauty and warm personality to sway him.

"After you adopted Ryan, did your marriage get better?" he heard himself asking, waiting for her answer even as he inwardly winced.

"No, not really. I actually was on the verge of asking for a divorce when he was killed."

Now *this* was news. Evidently she'd been successful at keeping this information out of the media, which meant, he reflected, that she most likely hadn't confided in anyone.

"Why?" he asked.

Expression troubled, Emily raised her caramel-colored gaze to his. "I don't know. Sometimes I think I wasn't meant to be married. The man I'd loved, the man I'd believed my husband to be, that person was entirely fabricated. Carlos kept his true self separate from me, from our marriage. Gradually, over time, bits and pieces came out. To be honest, I was secretly relieved when I learned he had mistresses."

Blindsided, Mac didn't understand. "Relieved? Why?"

"Because then I had something concrete on which to blame my marriage's failure. I had a rational excuse to leave."

Still he didn't get it. "If you were unhappy, then why'd you need an excuse? Why didn't you just go?"

Now she stared at him, looking incredulous. "We had a child. We were a family."

"And you wanted out. Are you saying you had to justify your own unhappiness?"

A brief quiver, the slightest hitch in her breathing, told him that his comment had hit home.

"Yes," she admitted. "I needed to justify wanting to leave him. Despite the lies and the illegal activities it turned out he was involved in, on the surface Carlos was a model husband. He didn't beat me—in fact, he treated me more like precious china. He provided well for us. We never wanted for anything."

"But you weren't happy."

She sighed. "That's not the issue. When there's a child involved, you don't just walk away and split up a family that easily."

God, he wanted to kiss her. Instead, he forced himself to think—really think—about her words. After all, he knew about the various trouble spots that could strike a marriage. He'd lived them. In fact, his wife Sarah had admitted she'd decided to get pregnant in a last-ditch hope of saving their marriage. The fact that she hadn't consulted with him first had actually made things worse—until the baby inside her became real.

Then, he had begun to believe that maybe she was right. Once they had a child together, everything would be all right. They'd work things out.

"That makes sense. I get that. But Emily," he continued, gentling his tone, "how could you not know what Carlos did? He was constantly in the news for one thing or another. How'd you rationalize his multiple arrests, the fact that the Feds had him on their radar?"

"Put like that," she said wryly, "I sound pretty stupid. But the short answer is I didn't know. Ryan kept me busy. I did a lot of charitable work for the animal shelter and a couple of other local charities. Whenever I happened to see the occasional news story, he always had a good explanation."

"How do you explain away being indicted for wire fraud? Or being the head of a large drug cartel?"

"*Suspected* head," she pointed out, even as she shook her head. "And he claimed the indictment was a business rivalry gone bad."

When he opened his mouth to speak again, she held up her hand, letting him see how her fingers trembled. "Look, Mac, I knew Carlos wasn't a good person. I guess I didn't want to let myself see exactly how bad he actually was. But once he was murdered, I had no choice."

They stared at each other for a moment in silence. Her agitation and frustration were nearly palpable, and again he struggled, hands fisted at his sides, to keep from touching her.

Seeing her like that, her glossy dark hair sticking up as if she'd just gotten out of bed, so sexy and slender and fragile-looking, he ached to gather her in his arms and hold her close. Though she tried so hard to be strong, he knew from personal experience that everyone had a breaking point.

The question he faced was this: Did he want to be the one who broke her or the one who helped her hold things together?

Things were coming full circle.

It all came down to this. Did he still believe Emily Gilley had knowingly stolen a baby—his child—named him Ryan and made him her son? Or because she wanted a baby so badly, had she turned a blind eye to her husband's worst crime? Was she as innocent as she appeared to be?

When he'd made the decision to come to Anniversary, his plans had been clear-cut and sharp: find out if Emily Gilley's Ryan was truly his son and go from there.

Now…he didn't know what to think. He'd spent many years in law enforcement and had always believed he had a good eye when it came to people. Every instinct he had kept telling him that Emily Gilley was exactly as she appeared—good, kind and loving. She didn't even appear to realize how her stunning beauty affected men.

Disgusted with himself, he swallowed. If he kept on letting his emotions—and frankly, his libido—control him, he'd eventually mess things up. And since Ryan was all he had left in this world to call his own, he couldn't let anything interfere with their reunion.

Of course, he still had to determine if Ryan was actually his son. This, he reminded himself sharply, must always be his focus—no matter how sweet and charming and sexy Emily might appear.

Emily had run out of words when her cell phone rang. Grateful for any distraction that would keep her from oversharing any more with Mac, she answered.

"Hello, Em!" Jayne Cooper's excited voice boomed into her ear. "I just wanted to remind you about tonight."

"Tonight?" Emily drew a blank. "What's tonight?"

Jayne laughed. "Surely you didn't forget. Tonight we're meeting at The Cheesy Pepper for girls' night. We've been planning this all week, remember?"

With all the craziness that had been going on, Emily had completely blanked on the fact that they'd made plans earlier in the week. "I can't," she said unequivocally, filling her friend in on what had happened.

"I heard some of that from Ed," Jayne told her. "And if anyone needs a break, it's you."

Emily couldn't even imagine trying to have fun after something like this—and said so.

"You need to unwind," Jayne insisted. "There's nothing better for that than a night out with your best friends."

"I could do dinner but nothing more. But—" and she meant this, sort of "—unfortunately, I haven't even booked a babysitter. And you know how hard it is to find a good one this late on a Friday." Since Jayne had two children herself, she'd know it was nearly impossible.

"You forgot to get a sitter?" Jayne asked, sounding a bit shocked. Then she clucked. "I'm sorry. Of course you forgot. You've certainly had a lot to deal with this week."

Relieved, Emily swallowed, trying to get words out past the sudden lump in her throat. "I'm so glad you understand," she began.

"Oh, I do. Completely. And that's why you need a girls' night out more than ever." Determination rang in Jayne's voice. "My husband is watching our two, and I'm sure he wouldn't mind one more. They're planning on ordering pizza. Bring Ryan over. He likes to play with Charlie. He'll have a blast."

Emily blinked. "I don't know…"

"Yes. You. Do. I'm not taking no for an answer."

Finally, Emily had no choice but to tell her friend the truth. "I'm afraid to leave Ryan. This nutcase seems to be targeting him."

"Sweetheart, you know Ed is a sheriff's deputy, right? He's fully aware of your situation. He won't let anything happen to your baby."

"I'd rather—"

Jayne bulldozed on as though Emily hadn't spoken. "Now bring Ryan over to my house around six. You don't have much time. And wear something cute. We are going out on the town."

"Dinner only," Emily protested weakly and too late. Listening to the click that meant Jayne had disconnected the call, Emily shook her head, trying to smile and failing miserably.

How could she do this? Go out with her friends and pretend everything was normal? Instead of what— sitting home alone jumping at every outside sound?

She sighed. Maybe Jayne was right. Perhaps a night with Tina and Jayne would help Emily quit worrying. After all, it couldn't hurt. And, as Jayne had pointed out, her husband Ed worked for the sheriff's department as a deputy.

While she was there, Emily resolved to ask him what he thought of Mac Riordan. She still wasn't sure she entirely trusted him.

"Earth to Emily," Mac said, startling her. Somehow, she'd managed to forget he was there. "Is there a problem?"

"No," she answered, debating whether or not to tell him her plans. Then, because he'd no doubt find out from Ed anyway, she filled him in on Jayne's call.

"I think that's a good idea," he said, surprising her. "You need to take a break from this craziness. Dinner and a drink with your friends might go a long way to helping you feel better. I don't know about you, but I always think more clearly when I'm relaxed."

Since he'd just voiced her own thoughts exactly, she considered him. "You don't think Ryan will be in any danger? Because if there's the slightest chance—"

"Ed can handle things. He's been a deputy for a long time."

Still she hesitated. "I don't know…"

He touched the back of her hand. Though his touch was light, she still felt a shiver of electricity. "If it'll make you feel better, I can go over there and hang out with him while you're gone. Two deputies are better than one."

Astonished, she looked up. His posture seemed casual and friendly, but he seemed to be keeping himself perfectly still, as though holding his breath waiting for her answer, which made absolutely no sense whatsoever.

"You'd do that?" she asked slowly. "Give up your Friday night to help Ed keep my son safe?" She couldn't believe it. While she could tell Mac was dedicated to his job, this went above and beyond.

"Of course." He grinned. "Actually, it would be a win-win situation. I don't have any plans, and I like the heck out of Ed. We could play cards or something."

With two deputies, her son would be safer at home than with her. And she really could use a break. Deciding, Emily slowly nodded. "I'll take you up on that. I have to pick up Ryan from school. Jayne wants us there around six."

Mac stood. "I'll be there around the same time."

Hyperaware of him, her skin prickled when he walked by. Even Emily's halfhearted attempt to rationalize that this was because of her lingering suspicion fell flat. She knew—and she'd be lying to herself if she pretended otherwise—that something about him attracted her in a way no man had done for years.

Studying him from under her lashes, she tried to analyze her reaction. He radiated confident masculinity, though in an entirely unselfconscious manner. Her husband had once been such a man—or so she'd thought. Only a lot of Carlos's confidence masked a bone deep, vicious insecurity. Somehow she doubted Mac Riordan had a single self-doubting bone in his broad-shouldered body.

Then she wondered why she even cared. All that mattered was finding the creep who'd been stalking her and Ryan. Once he'd helped her do that, she'd doubted she'd ever see Mac again, no matter how strong the attraction.

Showing him out, she watched as he walked to his car, unable to resist admiring his broad shoulders and the way his jeans fit his backside. She even liked the way he walked—a sort of take-the-bull-by-the-horns, no-nonsense stride.

Then, as he started the car and drove away with a

friendly wave, she chastised herself. The last thing she needed in the middle of all this craziness was to develop a crush on anyone, especially on the handsome sheriff's deputy assigned to help her.

Chapter 7

Once he'd put away his notebook and left her house, Mac drove home, unable to resist singing along to the music on the radio. With his heart light for the first time in months—hell, *years*—he felt as if he'd been given an amazing, stupendous gift. In fact, he couldn't believe his luck. Emily had essentially given him a free pass to spend time getting to know his son.

He shook his head, grinning like a fool. His son. Even though he didn't have proof—only a DNA test would be able to prove that—he knew in his heart the truth. Ryan was his. And whether Emily had knowingly stolen him or not, nothing could change that.

Calling Ed, he gave his coworker a heads-up. The poor guy sounded, while a bit bewildered, really happy to have company while he babysat. When Mac mentioned a game of Texas Hold 'em, Ed grew even more enthusiastic. He volunteered to go to the store and get chips and dip in preparation for guys' night in.

Briefly, both men discussed the chance of the stalker putting in an appearance. Neither felt this was even a remote possibility, though they would be on their guard just in case.

Hanging up, Mac drove home. Now all he had to do was grab something to eat and then mentally prepare himself for the night. Nervous, anxious and excited all at once, his stomach doing flip-flops, he wondered if he'd even be able to choke down some dinner.

This news was so momentous that he could scarcely keep it to himself. Inside his living room, he paced, trying out a dozen different scenarios and rejecting each one. He'd simply have to play this by ear.

Taking out his cell phone, he toyed with the idea of calling Joe but decided at the last minute against it. He wasn't ready to talk about this—not now, not yet, while everything was still so fragile and new. He'd give the relationship with Ryan time to develop before he'd feel safe to share details with anyone else. Since Joe was his best friend, Mac knew his former partner would understand.

He felt a smudge of remorse for hiding the truth from his best friend. Soon, he'd remedy that. He knew Joe would be overjoyed when he learned Mac had not only met his son but was getting to know him, too.

Humming softly under his breath, Mac fixed himself a sandwich and washed it down with a diet soda. He wished he'd asked Emily what kind of toys Ryan liked but then remembered his brief foray inside the boy's room and smiled. He'd run by the store on his way to Ed's later and pick up some small gift for his son.

* * *

Friends, Emily thought happily, were one of life's greatest blessings. In New York, she hadn't made too many friends—at least not genuine ones. Most of the people who attached themselves to Carlos Cavell and his wife only hung around for the status or because they wanted something for themselves.

After Carlos's death, the truth of this had been hammered home when all of the women she'd hung out with suddenly didn't answer their cell phones or return her calls. Her friends here in Anniversary were one of the many reasons Emily valued her life in the small town.

Guilt stabbed her as she wondered if it was wrong to be so happy about having some time with Jayne and Tina, sans child. Though intellectually she knew this respite from worry was a good idea, she couldn't shake the guilt. Any other time she would have acknowledged that she deserved this—she put in her time both as a full-time worker and a mommy.

But any other time, she didn't have some wacko after her for an imaginary crime. She could have withstood this, she thought, if only the stalker hadn't involved her son.

Then she thought of Mac Riordan with his quiet sense of purpose, and her doubts silenced. Ed and Mac wouldn't let anything happen to Ryan, and she needed to let go of her guilt and enjoy her time with her friends.

This resolved, she mentally reviewed the meager contents of her closet. It had been so long since they'd had a girls' night out that she could hardly think about what to wear. One aspect to this was the way she'd need to go about preparing.

A night out on the town in tiny Anniversary, Texas, was quite a bit different than a night out in Manhattan, New York. Here in Anniversary, cowboy boots and jeans were the perfect going-out attire. She really liked the fact that she didn't have to wear stilettos and a short dress. She also loved that she didn't have to be "on," worrying about a stray photographer or a flash going off in her face. Being married to one of New York's most notorious men had made her a minor celebrity there. Here, she was just plain old Emily Gilley, a single mom who worked in the vet's office.

And, she thought to herself with a smile, she had two of the best friends a woman could ever want.

With the simple acceptance of childhood, Ryan was unsurprised to see her early for the second day in a row.

"Everything all right, Mommy?" he asked, climbing into the car.

"Yep," she answered, chucking him under the chin. "How'd you like to go play with Eva and Charlie tonight while Mommy and Jayne go out?"

"For dinner?" He frowned, apparently not sold on the idea.

When she nodded, his frown deepened. "Will I get to eat first?"

"I think Ed is ordering pizza."

Just like that, his little face cleared. "Oh, okay. As long as Ed makes Eva share with me and Charlie."

That settled, she waited until Ryan had finished buckling himself in and drove home to plot what to wear. Despite Jayne's and Mac's reassurances, she vacillated between wanting to call off the entire night and being excited at the idea of taking a few hours to catch up with friends.

In the end, she decided to go through with her plans. Both she and Ryan could use a diversion.

A couple hours later, she pulled up to Jayne's small

ranch house with a hyperactive Ryan bouncing in the car seat. He'd gotten more and more excited the longer he considered the prospect of a night playing with his friend Charlie. She almost pitied Ed and Mac having to deal with him.

With Mac's patrol car parked in front of the brick house and Ed's in the driveway, the place looked well guarded. Her heart lightened a few more degrees, and she began to think she might be able to enjoy herself after all.

As soon as she turned the engine off, Ryan unbuckled himself, yanked the door open and took off running for the front door. Following behind at a more sedate pace, Emily couldn't help but grin. So much for worrying that her son would miss her.

Jayne met her at the door, giving her a big hug as Ryan tore past. "You didn't tell me Mr. Tall and Delicious was coming over," Jayne whispered.

Concerned that maybe she should have asked her friend's permission, Emily grimaced. "Sorry. I'm pretty sure he said he was going to clear it with Ed."

"He did." Jayne hugged her. "I was just teasing."

Aware of her red face, Emily shrugged. At Jayne's knowing look, she shook her head. "He's helping protect Ryan. Nothing more, nothing less."

"Oh, yeah? Then why are you blushing?"

To her consternation, Emily felt her face grow hotter. It was for no good reason, either—that is, if she didn't count the persistent smoldering attraction that always seemed to be simmering between them. "Are you ready?" she asked, pretending to ignore Jayne's expectant expression. "I'm starving."

"Sure." Jayne shrugged. "Let's go say goodbye to

the rug rats, and then we'll go pick up Tina. I'm glad she didn't have to work tonight."

As they walked into the living room, Emily saw Mac and Ed sitting side by side on the sofa, while Ryan had joined Charlie in front of the big-screen TV, already engrossed in a video game. Eva, a few years older, sprawled on the armchair, reading a book.

Mac's gaze swept over her, and he grinned. Giving her a thumbs-up, he winked.

Emily felt her blush deepen. Next to her, Jayne laughed. "If you two can quit making googly eyes at each other, we wanted to say bye. We've got to go pick up Tina, and then we're heading out."

Pushing himself up off the sofa, Ed crossed the room and gave his wife a quick kiss on the lips. Glancing at Emily, he smiled. "Don't you worry any, hon. Ryan's in good hands."

Face still flaming, she smiled back. "Thanks."

"Are you ready?" Practically bouncing on her feet, Jayne was clearly eager to go.

"Just a second. Bye, Ryan," Emily said. Her son didn't even turn and look at her. Instead, he lifted his hand in a backward wave without taking his eyes off the video game.

As she and Jayne left the room, Emily sighed. "I suppose it's good that he's not going to miss me at all, right?"

Her friend gave her a curious look. Then apparently realizing Emily was serious, she smiled and gave her a shoulder bump. "Why should he? Ryan and Charlie are friends. They'll have a blast tonight. Poor Eva. It's going to be guys' night at my house—video games, pizza and cards. Though as long as they leave her alone and let her read in peace, she'll be fine."

Emily nodded, saying nothing.

Apparently, her nervousness showed. After they got in the car, Jayne reached over and gave Emily a quick hug. "And you'll be all right, too. I promise. Now relax and let yourself have fun."

"I'll try," Emily said, meaning it.

Taking his cue from Ed, Mac kept his demeanor relaxed and easygoing, though his insides were churning with emotion. He tried not to focus too much on Ryan, though he couldn't help but be hyperconscious of the boy who was his son. He'd trashed the idea of buying a gift, realizing such a gesture might be viewed with suspicion.

While Charlie and Ryan battled it out in their video game and Eva read, Ed got out a deck of cards and a couple of beers. The house had an open layout, and the kitchen table had a clear view of the living area. The two men played a few games of poker, using chips instead of money. They talked shop, though since Ryan was present, they didn't touch on the Emily Gilley stalker case. Mac found the complexity of the other cases interesting, amazed such crimes occurred in a small town like Anniversary.

When the pizza arrived, Ed made the boys turn off the TV and Eva put her book down and join them at the table. They had three large pizzas, probably too much, but Ed said he'd rather have extra food than not enough.

To Mac's surprise, Ryan climbed into the seat next to him.

"Hi," Ryan said, reaching for a slice of cheese pizza.

"Hi, yourself." Mimicking the boy's motions, Mac chose a piece of the same pie.

Taking a big bite, Ryan chewed, studying Mac all the

while with a string of cheese hanging from his mouth. "Are you my mommy's boyfriend?" he asked.

Mac nearly choked. He glanced at Ed, saw from the other man's grin that he'd get no help there and managed to swallow. "No," he said, hoping he sounded more nonchalant than he felt. "I'm trying to help your mom catch the bad guys who broke into your house."

Snagging another huge bite, the boy nodded. "I think it's the same people who were after my dad."

Hearing another man referred to as Ryan's dad didn't hurt as much as he'd expected. Again, Mac exchanged a glance with Ed. "You remember people being after your father?"

With a shrug, Ryan helped himself to another slice. At the same time, Charlie went for the exact same one. Even though there were several other identical pieces to choose from, a minor scuffle ensued, mostly consisting of shoving and elbowing and Charlie yelling.

"Enough." Ed didn't shout, but he didn't have to. The authority in his voice was sufficient to instantly quiet the boys. Mac viewed his coworker with admiration as Ed admonished the children to be nice and share.

Then, with both boys quietly munching on their pizza and Eva still ignoring them all, immersed in her food, they happily continued the meal. Ed glanced at Mac, then at Ryan and did a double take.

"That's so weird," he said, chuckling. "You and Ryan look enough alike that you two could be related."

Mac froze. With an effort, he pasted what he hoped was a surprised look on his face and turned, pretending to study the boy. Ryan gazed back at him, a surprisingly serious look in his nearly identical blue eyes.

"I don't know. Maybe." Mac shrugged, as if the issue was of no importance, as if his heart wasn't pounding.

"We have the same color eyes," Ryan said. "Blue." Sounding proud, he looked from Mac to Ed and back again. "My mom's eyes are brown."

"So you know your colors," Charlie scoffed. "Big deal. I learned those in preschool."

"So did I." Ryan punched his arm, no doubt meaning to emphasize his point.

"No more of that." Ed's stern voice stopped Charlie from sure retaliation. "If you want to play some more of that video game, you two need to eat your pizza peacefully."

"Fine," Charlie huffed, again reaching for another slice at the same time as Ryan. But as it looked like another mini-battle would break out, a sharp look from Ed had each boy taking separate pieces and eating them in silence.

"I have to admire your parenting skills," Mac said after the children had finished eating. The boys had resumed playing their game, and Eva had retreated to her room with her book.

"Thanks." Ed grinned. "It comes with the territory."

"I don't know." For the first time since he'd seen a resolution to his obsessive quest to regain his son, he questioned whether or not he'd be able to be a good father.

"You just do what your dad did with you, that's all." Stretching, Ed gathered up the empty pizza boxes. "As long as it worked, that is."

"I didn't have a dad." Though Mac didn't usually talk about his past, he needed answers or reassurance and thought Ed would be the man to help him. "My mom raised me alone. She died of ovarian cancer right after I got married when I was twenty-five."

"Wow. I'm sorry to hear that."

Mac shrugged. "It was a long time ago."

"You never even had a stepdad?"

"Nope." He smiled to show Ed it really wasn't a big deal.

"Okay." Jamming the pizza boxes in the large trash can, Ed wiped the table off with a paper towel. "I guess it doesn't matter since you and your wife never had kids, right?"

Rather than commenting, Mac began to shuffle the cards. "Let's play."

"So…" Tina took a sip of her mango margarita before leaning forward to peer at Emily. "What's going on with you and Mac Riordan?"

Emily blinked, ignoring how her heart leapt into her throat at the mention of his name. "Going on? Nothing. He's working for the sheriff's office and trying to find out who's stalking me."

Tina and Jayne exchanged a meaningful look while Emily felt her face grow hot—again. What the heck was wrong with her?

"I think it might be a bit more than that," Jayne pointed out gently. "After all, he's at my house right now with Ed, helping watch Ryan."

"He is?" Clearly intrigued, Tina's eyes widened. "Do tell."

Both women eyed Emily expectantly.

"There's nothing to tell. Seriously." Grabbing a chip from the basket in the middle of the table, she plunged it into the bowl of warm *queso* and ate it slowly before reaching for another.

"Emily." Placing her hand on Emily's arm, Tina leaned close. "He's hot, he's single and obviously he has eyes for you. Why not give him a chance?"

Looking down, Emily tried not to react. She'd have to be a fool to get involved with another man after what Carlos had done to her. But they didn't know that. After all, Jayne and Tina meant well. These women were her friends.

"I'm not in the market," she said lightly. "Look what happened when I agreed to go out with Tim Keeslar."

Tina groaned. "Okay, so that was a mistake. I'm sorry for setting you up with him."

"I know Mac was trying to locate him," Jayne put in. "He wanted to ask him some questions and make sure he doesn't turn out to be your stalker."

"He's not my stalker." Emily knew she sounded weary, but she couldn't help it.

"How do you know?"

"I don't, but I think he just really liked me and I wasn't ready to be in any sort of a relationship. And I'm still not," she said pointedly.

"Ah, but this is totally different." Tina grinned. "Tim Keeslar is no Mac Riordan. I can't believe you don't find him attractive."

Ignoring the way her face heated, Emily grabbed another chip. "I didn't say that. He's a very handsome man. I'm just not in the market. I already told you to go for it, Tina, if you think he's so hot."

Laughing, Tina had the grace to look abashed. "He's not interested in me. I already tried flirting with him, and he had about as much interest in me as I have in Wendell Wayne Barnes."

Since everyone in Anniversary knew Wendell Wayne believed himself madly in love with Tina, despite the fact that he was thirty years older and looked like he never bathed, this cracked Jayne up. Emily even had to laugh, glad she'd rerouted the conversation away from her love life—or lack thereof.

The waiter chose this moment to bring their sizzling fajitas: chicken for Emily, beef for Jayne and shrimp for Tina.

"Corn and flour tortillas," he announced. "Do you need anything else, ladies?"

In unison, they shook their heads. Both Jayne and Tina had to wipe their eyes; they'd been laughing so hard.

Silence fell for a moment while the women dug in.

But Tina wasn't done. She'd barely loaded her tortilla with meat, cheese, guacamole and sour cream and taken a bite when she looked at Emily. "Now you are aware that Mac Riordan is about the hottest man in town, right?"

"She's right," Jayne chimed in. "Except for my husband, that is. What she's trying to say, honey, is if you're holding out for something better, you're wasting your time. Mac's it."

"Can we change the subject, please?" Emily kept her voice friendly but firm. "I need this night out to forget about my problems, not rehash them."

Jayne raised one perfectly arched brow. "Are you saying Mac is a problem?"

"No. Yes. Oh, stop." Swatting her friend, Emily grabbed a second corn tortilla and began loading it up with chicken, refried beans, rice and shredded cheese. She bit in, rolling her eyes. "This is heaven."

They finished their meal and a second margarita each, except for Jayne since she was driving.

"One order of sopaipillas, please," Tina told the waiter. "And three forks."

With a nod, he hurried off to get their dessert. As

they watched him go, Jayne looked beyond him and frowned.

"Check out that woman over there, near the tortilla-making machine," she said, lowering her voice. "Do you think she's a hooker?"

Both Emily and Tina turned to look. The instant Emily saw the heavily made-up bleach-blonde in the skin-tight dress, her heart sank. Desiree was sitting in a corner booth with Franco, enjoying giant margaritas and laughing, heads close together.

Closing her eyes, Emily drew on every ounce of inner strength she possessed to keep herself from reacting—at least physically.

Though her heart raced, she managed to chuckle while Tina and Jayne thoroughly trashed Desiree. But when they switched to speculating about the hunky man with her, Emily felt sick.

Still, she had no choice but to remain in place, pretending to have a good time. At least with her back to the other woman, there was still a chance Desiree wouldn't notice her—not so if Emily got up to leave, though.

Cursing under her breath, Emily tried to steer the conversation to something else, bringing up Mac out of sheer desperation. To her relief, her friends eagerly latched on to that topic, until Desiree and Franco got up to leave.

"Look at those shoes," Tina breathed. "How can she even walk in them?"

Counting to three so the other couple would be well on their way to the door, Emily finally turned to look. She caught the back of them, noting that Franco had gotten rid of his fake wheelchair.

Once they'd left the restaurant, despite her roiling

stomach, Emily struggled to at least pretend to enjoy the rest of the night. Neither Jayne nor Tina appeared to notice anything was wrong, which meant her acting abilities must have improved.

Still waiting on the sopaipillas, Jayne's cell phone rang. She answered and listened before muttering something unintelligible and ending the call.

"Is there a problem?" Emily asked, immediately concerned about Ryan.

"I'm not sure," Jayne said slowly. "That was Ed. He got a phone call from someone who claims to be Ryan's parent. He said he couldn't tell if the caller was a man or a woman. Do you know who the people are who gave him up for adoption?"

Dumbfounded, Emily stared. "No. But this is exactly what's been going on…the letters, the break-in. And I got several hang-ups at work, the day I was out after the break-in."

"Are you all right?" Both women viewed her, concern written all over their faces.

"No." With her throat closed up, Emily found it difficult to speak.

"Oh." Obviously troubled, Jayne looked down at her plate before raising her eyes to meet Emily's. "I think we'd better skip dessert and head home."

"Right." Emily jumped to her feet, feeling as though her heart would pound right out of her chest. Had Desiree made the call after leaving the restaurant? "What did this person say? Did he or she threaten Ryan?"

"No. Oddly enough, the only threat was made toward Mac."

"What?" Emily couldn't believe it. This was a new twist. "I don't understand."

"Well, despite your protests that you and Mac aren't

involved, I'm guessing Ryan's biological parent thinks you are. And this doesn't appear to make him or her very happy."

"That makes no sense. Even if we were—and we're not—what does that have to do with Ryan?"

Until now, Tina had remained silent, but now she moved forward and put her hand on Emily's shoulder. "Maybe it's the idea that you two are going to make a family with Ryan. Stalkers are usually crazy," she said. "Most times their actions don't make much sense."

Jayne signaled for the check. "She's right. This guy—or gal—could be convinced that you, as well as your son, belong to him. Any male seen as threatening this fantasy would be considered a danger."

"Which is why he or she threatened Mac." Emily's dull voice mirrored the ache beginning to thrum inside her skull. She fidgeted while Jayne paid the bill, promising to reimburse her friend later.

"The question I have now," Jayne said as they hurried out to her car, "is what is Mac going to do about it?"

Chapter 8

Staring blankly while Ed relayed in a voice too low for the boys to hear exactly what the caller had said, Mac clenched his jaw. Who was this person claiming to be Ryan's biological parent? This reminded him yet again that while he was ninety-nine percent certain Ryan was his stolen infant, apparently someone else believed differently. Until a DNA test was run, there'd be no way to know for certain. Gut instinct didn't count.

"And you didn't recognize the voice?" Mac asked.

"No. I couldn't even tell if it was a man or a woman. Whoever it was used some kind of voice-distortion software, like the kind you can get over the internet."

Mac cursed.

"Jayne and the girls are on their way home," Ed continued. "I hated to mess up their night, but this is too important to ignore."

"I agree." Mac didn't have to feign his anger. For the

first time, he wondered how accurate Joe's information had been. Was it actually possible someone else was Ryan's birth parent? Like, as Emily had mentioned, one of Carlos's mistresses?

If that turned out to be the case, he thought with a weariness that struck deep inside all the way to his soul, that meant his real son was still out there somewhere. And the likelihood Mac would find him five years later was highly improbable.

"I've contacted the phone company," Ed was saying. "They're running a trace on the call. If we can get an originating number, we'll know where the perp's hiding out."

"Right." But Mac knew what the trace would yield— a disposable cell phone, a "burn" phone, which was untraceable.

He squinted at Ed. "What did Jayne say?"

"They were going to leave right away and head home."

"Do you know how much she told Emily?"

Ed stared back. "Probably everything. Why?"

He glanced at the boys, still engrossed in their game. "Just wondering how much interference to run."

Ed grimaced. "I know what you think, but from what I've seen of Emily Gilley, she'll be cool as ice around her kid. You don't have to worry about that."

"I never did get a hold of Tim Keeslar," Mac groused. "The manager at the parts store he owns said he was on vacation. I checked his house, and no one is there."

"If he went out of town, he went salmon fishing up in Alaska. He goes every year about this time. But he should be back by now."

"Good. I'll try him again tomorrow," Mac said.

A moment later, the front door opened, and the

women rushed into the room. Jayne and Tina immediately crossed to the kitchen to join Ed and Mac. Emily instead walked calmly over to where the boys still sat transfixed in front of the TV.

He watched while she bent over and calmly kissed Ryan's cheek, murmuring something in his ear.

"I don't want to go home yet," Ryan whined.

Straightening up, she crossed her arms. "Now, please."

Amazingly, Ryan put down the controller and jumped up, following his mother without further protest. She came over to the group of adults, hugging Jayne and Ed and kissing Tina's cheek.

When she reached Mac, she stopped and held out her hand. "Thank you for your help tonight," she said, her touch as cool as her polite and distant voice. "Ryan and I are leaving now."

Before he could even frame a response, she turned her back to them, marching toward the front door. Sensing something was up, but not sure what, Ryan trotted along at her side.

After he cast a quick look of apology at Ed and the others, Mac rushed after her. He caught her just as she yanked the front door open and stepped outside.

"I'm going with you," he said, his tone leaving no room for argument.

She didn't even turn around. "Fine," she said, her voice so emotionless that it told him exactly how frightened she was inside.

His chest squeezed. How he wished he could protect her from this, from all of what was coming.

"Are you okay to drive?" he asked, trying to sound as if he only spoke because of his part-time profession as deputy.

"I only had one margarita," she said, her back ramrod straight, the line of her neck graceful. "And maybe one sip from my second. Plus I ate. I'm fine."

"Good. I'll follow you in my car."

Her only response was to dip her head in a curt nod.

When they got to her place, the motion-detection lights came on. Parking in front of the garage, he made her wait inside her car while he checked out the perimeter. Everything was still locked up tight, exactly as she'd left it.

He soon returned to her and rapped on the driver's side window. "All clear."

She got out slowly, with an instinctive grace he couldn't help but admire. Ryan, now sleepy, appeared to be in no hurry to go anywhere. She had to coax him, finally standing aside and letting Mac pick him up and carry him into the house.

"This way," she said, her voice low, leading the way to Ryan's room. "Just put him on the bed."

Once he'd complied, she began the process of getting the groggy five-year-old out of his clothes and into his pajamas. "We've still got to brush our teeth and wash our face and hands," she said. "Come on, Ryan. Help me out here."

Though Mac ached to assist her, he remained in the doorway, pretty sure she wouldn't appreciate his help. When she finally remembered him standing there, she flashed him a quick and polite smile.

"Why don't you go wait in the living room? Help yourself to a drink. I'll join you in a few minutes."

Eyeing her bending over the boy who might be his son, jaunty wisps of hair framing her heart-shaped face, he felt a peculiar sort of catch in his chest. Careful to reveal nothing in his expression, he simply nodded and moved away to do as she'd asked.

After rummaging through her refrigerator and locating a diet cola, he prowled around the living area, struck again by how completely at home he felt there. He'd lived in a lot of places since Sarah had died and he'd sold their house, unable to bear living with the memories. Most of them had been temporary, and none of them had ever made him feel at home.

Even the small place he'd purchased here in Anniversary felt like an impersonal mockery of everything he'd hoped it would be. At the end of a winding dirt road the frame house had looked to him like something out of a Norman Rockwell painting. He'd felt the impact, the raw wanting in his gut the first time he'd seen the place and known he had to have it. He'd been hopeful that this would finally become his home.

However, since moving in, he'd only unpacked a few boxes and done absolutely nothing to fix it up. Once again, he felt like a stranger in his own home, which told him this came from within him.

Shaking off the uncharacteristic melancholy, he took a seat on the edge of her couch. Then, restless, he got back to his feet and resumed prowling.

"Hey." Her soft smile told him she had no idea how sensuous her husky voice sounded. "Thanks for coming with me. He's asleep now."

"Does he usually go to bed this early?"

Glancing at her watch, she grimaced. "On school nights, yes. Since tomorrow is Saturday, I normally let him stay up later. He must have been really tired."

He studied her heart-shaped face and felt the familiar tug of desire. He wanted to kiss her. The urge to taste her lips again came out of nowhere, buffeting him like a sudden storm, taking him completely by surprise. Staring at her, he saw her pupils darken to chocolate and knew she felt it, too.

Their gazes locked. He could have sworn something intense passed between them. Heart pounding, he took a shaky breath, debating. Then her expression locked down and she moved away, answering his question without him even having to ask it.

With her back to him, she spoke, her voice hard and tight. "I saw Desiree and Franco tonight at The Cheesy Pepper. He was walking, not using a wheelchair."

He froze. "Why didn't you tell me that earlier?"

Arms crossed, she spun around to face him. "There was too much going on. The phone call…" Her voice broke, and he realized how perilously close to breaking she was.

Desperately trying to distract her, he said the first thing that came to mind. "Your house looks great. This is exactly how I wish my place looked."

"Thanks." She gave him a ghost of a smile that wobbled on the edges. "I don't have a lot of money, so I did the best I could. This is sort of how I imagine a basic suburban family home would look."

He focused on one word. "Imagine? You don't know? Where'd you grow up, on a farm?"

Her lush black lashes swept down to cover her eyes. "No, not exactly." Her tone told him to drop the subject. Feeling as if he were a treasure hunter, he didn't want to. As distractions went, this was a doozy.

"No farm, no suburbia. Hmm." Scratching his chin, he pretended to consider other alternatives. "A commune?"

His pitiful attempt at a joke didn't make her crack even the barest of smiles. Instead, she shook her head.

Though her expression was serious, at least she no longer appeared on the verge of collapse.

"If you really want to know, I grew up in an orphanage. I wasn't lucky enough to be adopted like Ryan."

He blinked. This floored him. In all the information he and Joe had put together, neither man had seen anything about that. Her husband Carlos must have used his considerable influence to bury that bit of information about his wife's past, though why, Mac didn't know.

"I'm sorry," he said. "I didn't mean to bring up old wounds."

She shrugged. "Don't be, it was a long time ago, and I'm over it."

Truly curious, he studied her. "What was that like?"

Something changed in her expression—not a total shutdown but close. "I don't..."

"Of course you don't have to tell me if you don't want to," he told her, his voice gentle, aching again to touch her. "I've never even been inside an orphanage. I can't even imagine how it must have been."

Eyeing him, she fingered a silky tendril of hair. "Living there wasn't that bad. I mean, it was all I knew. The hard part was staying there when a lot of the other kids got adopted or went to foster homes."

"And you didn't?"

"No." She didn't bother to hide the hurt in her caramel eyes. "I was a sickly child. Rheumatic fever, various infections—you name it, I had it. For that reason, they always passed me over. I didn't understand. At first, I though it must have been because I was bad, so I was super well behaved. Then, as I grew older, I went the opposite way and rebelled."

She grimaced. "In retrospect, I'm lucky I didn't end up in jail or worse."

"How long did you live there?"

"Until I was eighteen. That's how the system works. Once you age out, you're on your own. Luckily, I had a job at a fast-food place, and I'd been smart enough to save up some money, so I was okay."

The records Joe had dug up had indicated she'd married Carlos at twenty. "And then you met your husband."

"And then I met my husband." She sighed. "We were married four years."

When he only nodded, unsure how to respond, she tilted her head, openly studying him. "How about you? What's your story?"

Though he usually didn't talk about his past, he'd opened up. He really couldn't do any less.

"The usual. I never knew my father. I was raised by my mother in Albany. Became a cop after college. Married fairly young." Swallowing, he knew his light-hearted tone was all wrong, but using it always helped ease the pain. "My wife died in a car crash a little over five years ago."

Moving toward him, she squeezed his arm. "I'm sorry."

He prayed she wouldn't ask about children.

"What about your mom?" she asked instead.

"She passed away when I was twenty-five. Ovarian cancer."

"Ouch." She winced. "I'm sorry."

"Me, too," he said and meant it. "But like you said, that was years ago."

Spreading his hands to keep from touching her, he grimaced. "Enough talking about the past."

"Tell me how the investigation is going," she said, the breathy hitch in her voice the only thing that told him she was just as affected as he. "Have you found out anything at all?"

Looking down, he took a moment to gather his thoughts. "On the adoption, no. I've got a friend working with the NYPD and a private investigator in Manhattan. But since your former husband was under investigation by the FBI, everything is locked up tight. I'm still working on that."

"Thank you." She still wouldn't look at him. "It's so weird that I can't find even the tiniest trail to tell me where my son came from. I know a lot of adoptions are closed and I could understand that, but I can't even find any record that Ryan even existed."

Inwardly wincing, his stomach tightened as he debated whether or not to tell her about the newborn baby who had been stolen from Albany Medical Center right around the time she'd adopted Ryan. How would she react, learning the baby she thought of as her own might have actually belonged to him?

Might was the operative word, he reminded himself. He still didn't know for certain.

His cell phone rang, a welcome distraction. It was Renee. He listened to what she had to say, answered in the affirmative and concluded the call. Emily had turned and watched him silently, her eyes huge.

"That was Renee," he told her. "While we haven't had any luck locating Tim Keeslar, who's apparently out of town on vacation, we have managed to locate the hotel where Desiree and Franco are holed up. I'm on my way to meet Renee there now."

She nodded. "There's no point in worrying about Tim. If he's gone, he couldn't have broken into my house."

"True, but we have no idea when he left or if he is

even gone. And even if he didn't break into your house, he could have sent you the letters and made the phone calls." Her next words made him pause.

"Only if he somehow imagines he's Ryan's biological father," she said, "which I'm sure he does not. So cross him off your list."

He'd been a cop for so long that her words made him suspicious—almost as if she cared about this guy and didn't want him to be a suspect. An unfamiliar emotion twisted inside him. Without giving himself time to think, he reacted, crossing the space between them and, hands on her shoulders, pulling her close. "Why do you say this?"

Though she shivered, she didn't pull away. "Because when I went out with him, he wasn't real happy when he learned I had a son. I got the impression he was only interested in one thing, if you know what I mean."

Unfortunately, he did. Letting her go, he narrowed his eyes at the thought of another man touching her—any man. "I still want to talk to him."

She shrugged. "Keep me posted, please," she said, her tone a clear dismissal.

With a nod, he let himself out.

Driving to the address Renee had given him, glad he had time to calm his unruly body, he tried to push Emily from his thoughts and focus on the task at hand.

When he pulled up in the motel parking lot, the place looked deserted. Parking, he surveyed the area before getting out of his car. Well-lit and clean, this was a far cry from the sleazy place he'd pictured.

Of course, Anniversary was a much smaller town than Albany.

As he walked toward the motel office, a car pulled

up. Long, lean and shiny, the older model Cadillac would have looked at home in a classic car show.

His first thought was whoever drove this car wanted to be noticed. And when the front door opened and Chris Pitts, aka Franco DiSorinne, stepped out, the inference was that he had nothing to hide.

Turning, Mac hurried over. When Chris—or Franco—glanced up and saw him, he hesitated just long enough to allow Mac to reach him and draw his gun.

"I'd like to talk to you," Mac said, weapon up and ready. "Keep your hands in the air."

Franco didn't move. "Unless you're arresting me, I have nothing to say to you."

"Hands up," Mac barked. "Where's Desiree?"

Surprise flashed across Franco's face. "How do you—never mind. She's safe, and I'm not letting the likes of you bother her."

Renee would be here any minute now to provide backup. Mac just needed to keep the other man calm. "Why'd you do it, Franco? Pretend to be someone else so I'd hire you?"

Franco didn't react. Not even mild surprise showed in his stony expression.

"Come on, man." Mac tilted his head, though he kept his pistol up and ready. "I really liked you. I've done nothing to be treated that way. Why'd you do it?"

"Nothing against you." For the first time, Franco allowed himself a smug smile. "I needed cover, and your job opening provided it."

Now they were getting somewhere. "Cover? For what?"

But Franco wouldn't respond.

Another car pulled into the parking lot, headlights illuminating them. Renee turned on the blue and red lights before parking and getting out. She, too, approached with her weapon drawn.

"Where is she?" Renee barked. "Tell her to come out with her hands up."

Though Franco didn't move, he shifted his eyes toward the closest unit. Number 227. Perfect.

"I know where she is," Mac told Renee. "Cuff him, and I'll get her to come out."

"Hands behind your back."

Waiting until he saw Renee nudge a cuffed and furious Franco toward her squad car, Mac went up to the door of Room 227 and banged on it with an open fist. "Police. Open up."

Nothing. He glanced up at Franco and saw the other man smiling. But why? There were no back entrances to the motel rooms, so Desiree couldn't have escaped. Maybe Franco thought small-town officers wouldn't break into the room.

Taking a deep breath, Mac debated whether or not to try and kick in the door. Despite what television cop shows aired, such a move was never easy.

As he deliberated, a shot rang out.

"Get down," he yelled, dropping by reflex. Renee, however, wasn't so lucky. When he looked back for her, she was already on the ground, bleeding.

Immediately, he got on his radio and called dispatch for an ambulance as well as backup. But before he'd even finished speaking, the door to Room 227 opened and a woman who could only have been Desiree emerged crying, with her hands up.

Chapter 9

Ed Cooper took charge of the prisoners, booking Desiree with a charge of assault to a police officer with a deadly weapon. Franco was charged as her accomplice.

Mac followed the ambulance to the hospital. As far as he could tell, Renee's wound wasn't life-threatening, which was a relief. The bullet had grazed her shoulder, taking out a good-size chunk of flesh with it. Still, he wanted to be there for her and help in any way he could.

A few hours later, with Renee settled, her wound cleaned and bandaged, groggy with the meds she'd been given for the pain, he took his leave and headed down to the station to see what Ed had been able to find out.

"We're still holding them but not for long. They've both already lawyered up," Ed told him, with no small amount of disgust. "The only thing the girl would say was she shot Renee in self-defense."

"Self-defense?" Mac shook his head. "She shot a uniformed police officer."

"I know. It's weak. But that's what she's going with. How's Renee?"

Dragging his hand through his hair, Mac realized exhaustion had him seeing double. "She's okay. They're keeping her overnight, but I expect she'll be discharged tomorrow morning."

"Which is Saturday. At least we've got until Monday before their lawyer can get the judge to set bail." Ed grimaced. They both knew how this worked. Worse, Mac figured Franco and Desiree would vanish once they'd posted bond.

"I need five minutes," he told Ed.

"But—"

"Just go get a cup of coffee." Already walking away, Mac pointed in the direction of the break room. He didn't look back to see if Ed had done as he'd asked.

Franco and Desiree were being kept in separate holding cells until Judge Carrodine opened court on Monday morning and their attorney could petition for bail to be set. Mac chose to visit Desiree first.

She looked up when he entered the cell. Black mascara streaks ran down both cheeks as she regarded him suspiciously. "What do you want?" she asked.

Ignoring her question, he stared at her, unsmiling. "You're in a lot of trouble, you know."

"My lawyer will take care of this," she said without conviction. "He said not to talk to any of you."

Shaking his head, he continued to stare her down. "Why'd you do it, Desiree? Shooting a police officer is a pretty serious thing."

"I didn't mean to shoot her," she protested, apparently already forgetting her attorney's instructions.

"When you knocked on the door, I thought you were one of Franco's enemies."

She said this despite the fact that he'd identified himself as police loudly and clearly. Mac let that one go. "What do you want with Emily?" he asked casually. "She said you came to her house."

Desiree frowned, her worried expression replaced with one of contempt. "Carlos's stupid wife? She stole my jewelry, and I want it back. I need the money."

It was the same story she'd given Emily. If Desiree was after Ryan, she was doing a good job of pretending otherwise. Actually, Mac believed her. Women like her had no interest in children—their own or others. All they cared about was money.

This was exactly what Desiree had said. She was telling the truth, at least about that. Still…

"You came all this way for a necklace and bracelet?"

"And earrings." Sniffing, she swallowed. "These weren't ordinary diamonds, you understand? I saw the receipt. Carlos paid nearly two hundred grand for the necklace alone."

Damn. He knew Emily had sold everything to pay off her debts, but she hadn't mentioned very expensive diamonds. He'd have to ask her about that.

Turning, he exited her cell without another word and went next door.

Franco didn't even look up when Mac entered. One look at his clenched jaw and hunched shoulders told Mac he was barely holding back his rage.

"I might be able to get them to cut you a deal," Mac said casually, "but I'll need some information from you."

When Franco met Mac's gaze, he didn't bother to hide his anger. "Go away."

Staring him down, finally Mac nodded. "Suit your-self. Both you and your girlfriend are gonna do hard time for shooting a cop."

"I didn't shoot anyone," Franco snarled.

"Desiree says differently. She told me she was only doing what you told her to do." Mac felt no compunction about lying. He really didn't expect Franco to believe him. If the other man had been an associate of a mobster like Carlos Cavell, he'd been around the block enough times to know better.

Still, on the off chance that he was wrong, Mac crossed his arms and waited.

Finally, Franco spoke, glaring at him. "Tell me your deal, and I'll think about it."

"I need you to tell me what you want with Carlos Cavell's wife."

For an unguarded moment, Franco's expression mirrored his shock. Apparently, whatever he'd been expecting hadn't been this.

Jaw set, he looked away. "No comment."

Mac shrugged, feigning nonchalance. "All right, then. Let me know if you decide you want to talk about a plea."

Franco didn't respond, though Mac waited, silently counting to ten.

Then he let himself out.

Exhausted beyond reason, Mac knew he should get in the car, drive home and get some much needed sleep. Instead, though it was late and he thought she'd probably be asleep, he found himself pulling up in Emily's driveway.

Parking, he killed the engine and sat in the car. A light shone yellow from her kitchen window, and he used that as enough reason to get out and go tap quietly on her front door.

To his surprise, she opened it instantly, as though she'd been watching out the window and waiting for him.

About to speak, instead he pulled her into his arms and just held her, drawing comfort from the fresh shampoo-and-soap scent of her.

He didn't know how long they stood there, holding on to each other, but finally, as he swayed from exhaustion, she broke away and gently led him into the house, closing and locking the door behind her.

"What happened?" she asked quietly.

"First, I need to ask you about some diamonds. Desiree said the necklace alone was worth over one hundred thousand dollars."

She shook her head. "I didn't find anything like that."

"All right." He searched her face. "Desiree shot Renee."

Emily gasped. "What?"

Dropping into her chair, he relayed the night's events. She listened quietly until he finished, finally dropping to her knees alongside his chair.

"Is Renee going to be all right?"

He nodded, trying not to look at her mouth and unable to keep from remembering the explosiveness of the kiss they'd shared earlier. The rasp of his own breathing and the thump of his heartbeat mingled with hers. Despite his exhaustion and her earlier anger, the electricity between them still hummed in the air, too powerful... seductive...dangerous—especially now when his guard was so completely down.

He didn't move, couldn't move, even though he knew he was on the verge of doing something foolish.

Seeming to sense it, too, she moved restlessly against his leg. His mouth went dry as he watched her, realizing he'd never seen her as wildly beautiful. Desire stabbed deep inside him. Sensing his regard, she dragged her hand through her short, dark hair, biting her lip as she looked away.

He nearly groaned out loud. Hell, he wanted her. He wanted to bury himself inside her—right here, right now.

Again their gazes locked. She stopped moving and something—desire? heat?—flickered in her face. Motionless, her caramel eyes molten, she appeared to be waiting. He tried to throttle the dizzying surge of wanting, of need, but as she raised herself up onto her knees, he knew he fought a losing battle.

Roughly, he pulled her to him. Though she didn't resist, she trembled against his touch, settling on his lap. His body, already aroused, responded with a surge of heat.

"Emily?" he rasped, hoping she'd understand what he asked.

"Please. Hold me."

Though he knew he was in trouble if comfort was all she wanted, he did his best to simply hold her, though he knew she could feel his arousal pressing against her perfectly shaped bottom.

Turning to him, her full breasts flush against his chest, she clung to him, soft curves fitting him perfectly. When he slid his hand down her shoulder to the swell of her breast, he hesitated, heart hammering in his chest, hoping she wanted this as badly as he.

Apparently she did. She pressed her mouth against

his throat, where the pulse threatened to leap out of his skin. His heart lurched.

"Yes," she whispered. Then, pressing against him, she kissed him with a hunger that matched his, her soft, sweet lips more persuasive than any words could have been.

He let his mouth move over hers, devouring her, drinking her in, wanting more—so much more.

But was this...wrong? With his heartbeat pounding in his ears and heat blazing through his veins, he could scarcely think of anything but the feel and scent of her.

Emily, Emily. And though his mind told him to resist, his damn body refused to listen. She kissed him again with an unmistakable sense of urgency, and she took his hands, encouraging him to touch her.

Was he actually shaking? Pushing away the thought along with his doubts and his questions, he traced the hollow of her throat, the slope of her shoulders, her sides to reach the curve of her hips. He pulled her toward him, wanting her closer than was humanly possible. He knew she could feel just how much he wanted her. Despite his mammoth arousal, he tried like hell to maintain control. He wanted to let her be the one to choose how far this went.

As if he had the right to take this any further.

And then, she lifted her small, delicate hand and traced the outline of his erection, hard and rigid and ready, and he was lost. He tried to speak but only succeeded in a groan, and when she kissed him again, she continued to stroke him to madness with the certainty of her touch.

Though she already straddled him, when she began to move her softness against him, what little restraint he'd managed to hang on to completely and utterly vanished. Breathing harshly, he grabbed her wrist, holding her away.

"Stop," he bit out the word. "It's been way too long since I—"

"Shh." Brushing her lips against his, she got up and took his hand and led him into the bedroom. He went, dazed and tormented and too damn aroused to care.

Closing the door behind her, she kissed him again, this time warm and lingering and full of promise. Slowly she began unbuttoning her soft cotton nightgown, her seductive smile inviting him to help.

So he did—or at least, he tried. His fingers felt too big and ungainly. Fumbling with the buttons, he hoped he wouldn't tear the cloth, especially when she undid his belt.

A tangle of clothes and bodies, they undressed each other, each touch erotic, every kiss a sexy tease. She helped him pull his T-shirt over his head, trailing kisses along his chest, biting at his nipple. He sucked in his breath, self-control already shredded, while great shuddering waves of desire rocked him to the core.

Naked, bodies slick with perspiration and need, they came together as though they'd both been starving. And if he thought about it, he had.

Though he tried to be gentle, he could no more control his raging desire than he could a tornado. And she, she urged him on, apparently craving him as much as he did her.

When he would have gently eased them onto the bed, she grinned and pulled him instead, sending them sprawling, limbs intertwined in a sensual tangle.

They kissed again, his aroused flesh pressing into her soft belly then, as she moved, the warm apex of her womanhood. Bending his head, he caressed her breasts with his tongue, trying like hell to slow things down. He wanted to try to make this last.

But she had other ideas. Arching her back, she moaned, blindly reaching and capturing his hard-on with her hand, squeezing and moving her hands up and down seductively.

"Emily," he warned. "Easy."

Again she laughed, a husky sound of joyous sensuality. "I'm ready for you."

Knowing if he entered her now that he'd lose control, he used his finger instead, finding her wet and ready and hot—so hot. His body surged against her leg as she convulsed around his finger.

Damn. He wasn't going to be able to wait too much longer.

"I need you inside me," she breathed. Wiggling her body against his hand, she rose up against him and pushed herself down over the length of him, sheathing him deep inside her.

He bit back a moan. The pleasure was purely explosive. Slowly, he started to move, savoring the feeling. Thrashing, she bucked her hips, taking him in faster until he couldn't think, until there was only him and her—their bodies joined together.

"Mac!" Shuddering, she found her release, bringing him to his at nearly the same instant. The waves of pleasure seemed to go on and on, taking him by storm.

Finally, both spent, their naked skin moist and warm, they lay silent, holding each other, not speaking.

Sometime after that, she slept.

Eventually, after forcing himself not to think too hard about what had just happened, he did, too.

When he woke, the clock on the nightstand read 5:03 a.m. Quietly, he eased himself out of the sheets;

found his jeans, socks, shirt, shoes; and got dressed in the darkness.

Sneaking out before dawn was something he'd only seen in movies. This was another first in this bizarre chapter of his life.

Great. He'd done a lot of things in his past that he wasn't proud of, but this took the cake. He'd obviously been thinking with what was in his pants rather than his brain. How could he make love with a woman when he planned to be the one to completely ruin her life?

Emily was already wounded, shattered, and he'd begun to suspect she'd been wronged almost as much as he had. He had no business even becoming friends with her, never mind becoming her lover.

Worse, he already wanted to make love to her again.

Since he always tried to be honest with himself, he knew that despite his misgivings, he couldn't stay away from her. Even if he didn't have concern for Ryan's safety as an excuse, he genuinely *liked* Emily. He wasn't going to let anything happen to her—not on his watch.

And if it turned out Ryan was the infant who had been stolen from him five years ago, he'd try to work out some sort of visitation schedule rather than cutting her completely out of Ryan's life. He suspected both of them would need such an arrangement to stay sane.

Briefly, he tried to imagine the future. He couldn't. He knew what he'd like, knew too that such a thing would not be possible if he continued to pursue his planned course of action.

He needed answers, needed to know the truth.

Since right now he couldn't have them, he did the cowardly thing. He left Emily asleep in her bed without saying goodbye.

* * *

After Mac left, Emily lay still between the sheets with her eyes closed, doing some serious thinking. She'd always been a light sleeper, and she'd come awake the instant he slipped from the bed.

Though part of her longed to call him back to her, to wrap him in her arms and entice him to make love yet again, the rational side of her was glad he was going without her having to ask him to. She'd never let Ryan wake up to find a man in her bed, even Mac, whom Ryan liked and trusted. Maybe it would happen eventually, depending on how things played out, but not now—not while everything was still new and shiny and full of potential.

She wasn't even certain she wanted this. At this stage in her life—and in Ryan's life—she didn't need a relationship…especially with all the craziness going on with the stalker. Diamonds? It would be so ironic if all along her stalker had been after missing jewelry rather than Ryan.

It would be ironic and a blessing. While she knew nothing about diamonds, if she could believe with certainty that no one was after her boy, she'd finally be able to breathe again.

Until she knew for sure, she needed to focus on her son, make sure she gave him an ordinary, perfect life—the kind she'd always dreamed of for herself. Mac would only complicate things, but she'd be lying if she tried to pretend he wouldn't make a fantastic father.

And what little boy didn't need a father?

Turning around various possibilities, she punched her pillow and tried to will herself back to sleep. She didn't need this now. But what she needed and what she wanted, however, were two different things.

Mac Riordan had shown her how to desire again. Being with him had made her appreciate her femininity and reminded her of all the ways a male companion and lover could enrich her life.

But she knew better than anyone how this sort of sweet, sharp happiness could turn and plunge a knife into one's chest. Did she want to risk such pain, letting herself care about this man she barely knew?

After leaving Emily's, Mac headed home, showered and got ready to face the day. He stopped in a Patty's Coffee Shop and snagged breakfast and several cups of piping hot coffee. The food helped with the unsettled feeling roiling inside him.

Then as he'd done for years, he shoved his personal problems on the back burner and focused on his jobs.

After checking on his trucking business and wishing his former dispatcher, Chris Pitts, had been a real employee, he headed downtown to the hospital. He wanted to talk to Renee. This case, at least to him, had suddenly grown incredibly complicated.

With this latest wrinkle, was the stalker after diamonds, and if so, why the phone call from someone who, mistakenly or otherwise, believed he or she was Ryan's biological parent? With Carlos's former mistress and goon arriving in town together, Mac knew he needed to enlist help. He needed to talk to Renee first, and then he wanted to phone his buddy Joe back in Albany. He really hoped Renee could call in some outside law enforcement agency, maybe even the Feds.

Arriving at the hospital early that Saturday morning, he headed up to Renee's room, hoping she'd be awake and able to talk.

She sat up in her hospital bed, evidently having just finished breakfast.

"You got a minute?" he asked, stopping just inside her doorway.

"Sure." She dropped her fork and motioned to one of the visitor's chairs. Flashing him an amused smile, she shook her head. "Ed called and filled me in on everything. I'm glad we've got the shooter and her accomplice in custody. Nothing much is going to happen with that until Monday when Judge Carrodine goes back to work."

He nodded. "I know. I wanted a minute of your time."

"Sure." Leaning forward, she focused her direct gaze on him. "What's up?" With her short hair and larger-than-life bravado, she could have looked masculine but didn't. Instead, her shorn locks framed her heart-shaped face, emphasizing her femininity rather than detracting from it.

Mac had begun to consider her a friend. "About the Gilley case. Things are escalating. Not only does the stalker seem to think he or she is Ryan's birth parent but we've got two individuals in town who are part of Emily's past. They claim to be looking for some valuable jewelry. On top of that, we still don't know if any of these people tried to grab Ryan. I'm worried this person will try again." He took a deep breath. "I think Emily and Ryan are in danger."

Renee leaned forward. "Even with those two in custody?"

"Even so. Because I'm not a hundred percent convinced they are behind all this."

"Seriously? Crossing her arms and ignoring her bulky shoulder bandages, Renee frowned at him. "Who else could it be? If they really think Emily has their diamonds, maybe they wanted to grab the kid for insurance. You know as well as I do that holding him for ransom would be a viable way to get what they clearly think his mother has stolen."

"Too obvious. Neither one of them has even mentioned Ryan. But the caller did. This person—whoever he or she is—seems to think Emily stole his or her baby. They aren't happy with my involvement with her."

Expression thoughtful, Renee considered his words. "I don't know. Who are you thinking?"

"I'm not sure. Even though Tim Keeslar is supposedly out of town, I'd really like to talk to him. Because the stalker appears to be upping the intensity. I'm afraid he or she is going to make a move soon."

She'd gone utterly still. "How can I assist?"

Carefully, he spoke. "If you have any contacts inside the FBI that could help, that would be great. I'm gonna call Joe and get him working on this, as well. I still need information on the adoption."

"I agree. Because, unless Carlos Cavell stole this baby directly out of a hospital, there have to be records somewhere."

He held his breath, watching her to see if she knew she'd just stated what he believed to be the truth behind Ryan's appearance in Emily's life.

Continuing, she appeared oblivious. "I'll see what I can find out," Renee promised. "I should be out of here by lunchtime today, according to the doctor. I'll go directly to the office and get to work."

"While I appreciate that, I think you'd better rest." Mac patted her hand. "You just got shot, remember?"

"I wouldn't even call it that," she said, her mouth twisting wryly. "The bullet just grazed me. I'm fine.

As soon as they discharge me, I can go back to my normal life."

Mac managed a smile and a nod. Grabbing his car keys, he turned to go. Next up, he'd call Joe and get him to start working on the case. Joe had contacts inside the FBI who could really come in handy.

Letting himself out, he got in his car and pulled out his cell.

Joe picked up on the first ring, as though he'd been expecting the call. "Hey, buddy."

"Hey, yourself." Quickly he outlined the situation. When he'd finished, Joe whistled. "I had no idea things were heating up so much down there."

"Will you see what you can find out about Franco DiSorinne and a woman named Desiree Smith?"

"Is that her real last name?"

"It's what's on her ID."

"Okay. Will do. I'll be back in touch as soon as I find out something."

Hanging up, Mac allowed himself a slight smile. Joe always had his back, even though he now was two thousand miles away.

Satisfied he'd done everything he could for now, he shifted the cruiser into Drive and headed home. He'd spend a few minutes working on the trucking business before driving out to Emily's that afternoon to check on her.

Finally going back to sleep, Emily didn't get up for a few more hours, glad it was Saturday. When she woke, she wasn't too surprised to find herself missing Mac. Her body felt pleasantly sore from their lovemaking the night before.

Still, she was glad he'd left—especially since she

had an inquisitive son who would be sure to ask a lot of questions that she wasn't ready to answer.

Stretching lazily, she showered and then headed into the kitchen. She brewed herself a pot of coffee, heavily doctored it with cream and artificial sweetener and drank a cup while gazing out the back window.

Fear no longer ruled her life, she realized. For the first time she could remember, she actually felt anticipation and hope for the future. She felt strong and capable and ready to deal with anything. It'd been nice to know so many people in her new hometown had her back.

Especially Mac. Smiling, she shook her head. Baby steps, baby steps… She'd deal with her burgeoning feelings for him as they came.

When Ryan finally woke up around nine, she made blueberry pancakes, letting him eat them in front of the TV while he watched his cartoons, something he only got to do on Saturday mornings.

Pouring herself her second cup of coffee, she wandered out onto the patio. The bright blue, cloudless skies promised a hot day, but at this time of the morning, the outside temperature hovered in the low 80s.

Watching a squirrel raid one of the bird feeders, she took a seat in her favorite rocking chair, the one she'd bought from a display outside of a restaurant. She'd purchased the chair because it represented the kind of home she'd never had. It was one of the few possessions she'd brought with her to Texas. When she'd married Carlos, she'd hoped they could build that kind of home, but it hadn't worked out. So now, she and Ryan were working on making it on their own.

And now she was thinking of Mac. Again, images of him intruded into her world.

Last night had been…fabulous. She stretched her

body, aching in an unfamiliar yet recognizable way. Though the last thing she'd intended was to get involved with anyone, she couldn't deny their connection.

Thinking about more coffee, she wandered back inside. Still watching cartoons, Ryan glanced up at her and smiled. The sight of his freckled face filled her with joy. She collected his plate and took it into the kitchen to wash up.

She filled that morning with mundane tasks, trying not to think about the stalker, the two people currently being held by the sheriff's office or about Mac. She sorted laundry, started the wash, dusted and vacuumed, taking comfort in the ordinary domestic chores.

Outside, she heard the distinctive sound of the postal truck delivering the mail.

Walking out to get it, when she opened her mailbox, Emily frowned. Stuffed inside, along with the usual catalogs and bills, was a special delivery envelope addressed to her.

Seeing it, she froze. Since she hadn't ordered anything, she could only think it had been placed there by her stalker rather than the mail carrier.

Immediately, she called Mac.

"I'll be there in ten minutes," he told her, his deep voice sending warmth through her suddenly cold body. "I'm on the other side of town. Don't touch anything, okay? As a matter of fact, wait for me inside your house."

Agreeing, she hurried back inside, locking the dead bolt behind her.

Mac arrived in less than seven minutes, which meant he must have driven as fast as he could without using lights and sirens. He jumped out of the car, looking reassuringly big, his muscular shoulders straining the fabric of his shirt. As he strode up her sidewalk, his massive, purposeful presence quickened her pulse against all reason. Again, she flashed back to the night before, and her body flushed all over.

Chiding herself, she opened her door and met him halfway. It took every ounce of self-possession she had to keep from throwing herself into his arms.

Damn. She had it worse than she'd thought.

As he gazed at her, standing so close she could feel his body heat, she knew he was thinking about it, too. Her instinctive response to this realization was so powerful that she shivered and moved away.

She cleared her throat and tried to focus her scattered thoughts. "It's in the mailbox," she told him, her voice husky.

He nodded, his nearness still overwhelming. "Wait here," he ordered, his voice as rusty as hers had been.

Of course she couldn't. Hurrying along after him, she stood back a respectful distance while he opened the metal box and peered inside.

First he extracted her regular mail, handing the letters and catalogs and flyers to her. Then, working carefully, he removed the padded envelope marked Priority.

"So far, there's nothing to worry about. This came through the postal service," he told her, showing her the stamps. "The postmark shows it originated in Dallas. The postmark is smudged, but it looks like it was mailed yesterday or the day before. There's no return address."

She nodded. Raising her eyes, she found him watching her, the heat of his gaze making her sway toward him.

"What do you want to do?" he asked softly, the intensity in his voice palpable. "I can take it with me and open it in the sheriff's office, or we can cut it open right here, right now."

She forced a smile, aware she fooled neither of them. "I have to see what's inside."

Nodding, he pulled the precut tab. As he scanned the contents, his face shut down. Jaw clenched, eyes narrowed, he passed her the papers.

Instead of a note, there were photographs. Printed on an inkjet printer, the poor quality attested to inferior paper. Each and every one of them was of an infant, clearly in a hospital bassinet.

Gazing at them, at first she didn't comprehend. Then, when she did, she didn't understand. "These are...Ryan. At birth. Before I adopted him, I'm guessing."

"Yes." His voice, choked and raw, mirrored her emotions.

Disoriented, she looked up, trying to process not only this but Mac's reaction. Expression shuttered, he looked like a man in pain.

The photos proved that this stalker was truly her worst fear come to life. "Ryan's actual birth parent, someone who might not have willingly given him up." Just thinking of what that meant shattered her.

"Emily..." Mac reached for her, hand on her shoulder, his gentle touch oddly comforting.

"They mean to try and get him back, to take him away from me." Her fear and misery felt like a heavy weight pressing on her chest. "I can't let them do that. He's my son, my baby. He'll be lost without me. And I..."

Unable to finish the sentence, she bowed her head, the hot ache in her throat threatening to overwhelm her.

With a muffled curse, he pulled her close, wrapping her in his strong arms. Grateful, she let him hold her.

The suffocating sensation that had begun to tighten her throat eased somewhat.

"I don't think you need to worry about that," he said placing a light kiss on her forehead before holding her at arm's length. "We need to talk. There's something I have to tell you."

Folding her arms around herself as if the gesture could bring some warmth, she waited.

A muscle worked in his jaw. His eyes were tortured. She didn't understand why, but he seemed to be struggling with some sort of awful pain. "Though I don't recognize those pictures, I'm guessing they were taken right after Ryan was born, in the NICU."

Helpless, she nodded, willing him to continue.

"First off, you don't have to worry about Ryan's mother coming to try and reclaim him." The harshness of his voice spoke of great emotion, though she could read nothing in his shuttered gaze.

"How do you know this?"

Swallowing hard, he appeared to struggle to speak. "Because I believe Ryan's mother—" his voice cracked, despair darkening his features "—was my wife, Sarah. She died in a car accident on the same day he was born."

At first, she didn't comprehend. Then, ice spreading through her veins as she stared at him with dawning horror, she gasped. "That means you're—"

"Ryan's biological father."

Chapter 10

Emily felt sick. Raw emotion overwhelmed her. Backing away, she stumbled, nearly going to her knees. Terror shot through her, fear laced with fury. "Get away from me."

"Wait." He moved toward her, regret and longing warring in his eyes. Expression grim, he reached out as though to grab her. Somehow, she evaded him, rushing away from him, from the man she'd believed was her friend but who'd turned out instead to be her darkest enemy. She couldn't bear the sight of him.

"Get the hell away from me. You'd better leave, right now—before I call the police."

Since he was, in essence, the police, he didn't comment. Instead, he kept coming, his broad shoulders heaving as he tried to breath. "Listen to me. Please. I'm not your stalker. I swear to you I'm not. I don't know who that is."

"Then who are you?" she cried, despair and anguish twisting her insides.

"A man who's spent the past five years searching for his son." He let out a long, audible breath. "You have no idea what that's like."

She stared at him and she struggled with her confusion. Feeling as if the sky had turned to ice, then shattered and began crushing her, she shook her head. "I don't understand."

Regret flickered in his gaze. "I believe Ryan is my son. Five years ago, my wife was in a car wreck, and he was born prematurely." He cleared his throat, apparently trying to find the right words. "She died delivering him, and while I was burying her, my baby was stolen from the hospital."

Perplexed, she made a choked, desperate sound. "I'm sorry that happened to you, but what are your reasons for thinking Ryan is that child? If I remember right, your baby was born in an Albany hospital. I lived in Manhattan when I adopted Ryan."

"I haven't figured out all the details," he admitted, lifting his chin.

She no longer cared. "This is ridiculous. How dare you come here with this pile of—"

"It's true," he insisted.

Straightening her spin, she looked him in the eye. "I'm sorry you had such an awful thing happen to you, but you're mistaken about Ryan. He's not your missing child."

He took a step toward her, stopping only when she gave him a withering stare and yanked open the door.

"I think you need to leave," she said, crossing her arms.

"Ryan is my son." He lifted his chin.

"You have no proof."

"No, I don't." His mouth twisted. "Therefore, I'd like a DNA test. If you won't consent to one, I'll get an attorney."

Stunned and horrified, she could only stare. For a moment, she couldn't even breathe. "And then what?"

"And then we'll have to see." Posture rigid, he moved away. He didn't turn and look back at her before climbing into his car and leaving.

"I'll die before I let him take Ryan." Pushing her uneaten salad around in her plate, Emily let her dejected resolve show. She'd only thought things had been bad with the stalker and Desiree and Franco. This claim by Mac felt like the proverbial last straw.

Jayne eyed her, sympathy darkening her gray eyes. "Do you think he's your stalker, too?"

"No." Emily passed her hand over her eyes, wishing she could somehow make this all go away. "That's the weird part. This other person—I don't know if it's a man or a woman—also believes they are one of Ryan's birth parents."

"What about the mistress?"

"It could be her," Emily admitted. "And I still haven't figured out Franco's part in all this."

"Maybe he thinks he's the father, too."

Emily shook her head. "Anything is possible, I guess."

Leaning over, Jayne patted her hand. "Then a DNA test is the only way to go. It makes sense."

Finally, Emily gave up her futile attempt to get some nourishment. Her queasy stomach wouldn't allow her to eat anyway. "I can't risk it." Leaning forward, she decided to confide in her best friend. "I'm seriously thinking about packing everything up and leaving town in the middle of the night."

Jayne's mouth fell open. "No, you can't."

"It may be the only way I can keep my life from falling apart. I've got to protect Ryan."

Before she'd even finished speaking, Jayne had begun shaking her head. "Don't you want to know the truth? If Ryan really was stolen from Mac, then he is his son. There's nothing you can do to change that, and furthermore, Mac deserves to be in Ryan's life. It'll be best for both of them. Surely you two can work out some sort of arrangement."

She was right. Emily closed her eyes, still feeling sick. "So what do I do?" she whispered. "I'm so afraid."

"You have to believe Mac just wants a relationship with Ryan, not to take him away from you. He's not a monster."

"I don't know," Emily said bleakly. "He slept with me to get closer to my son."

Jayne gasped. "He…what? Seriously?"

"Yes." Emily closed her eyes. She dropped her lashes to hide the hurt. "I actually thought we might be beginning a relationship. I can't believe I was that stupid."

Jayne squeezed her hand. "Let's be proactive rather than reactive. Even though it's the weekend, let's get Ed involved and go talk to Renee. Don't forget that they still have Desiree and Franco in custody. I have a feeling she'll be in her office."

"Why?" Emily shrugged in resignation. "What good is that going to do?"

"First, I think you need to talk to Franco and Desiree yourself, in person. Second, we're going to make Mac tell Renee about his personal involvement in this. I'm betting she doesn't know." Jayne gave her a determined look. "We've got to get to the bottom of this once and for all."

She nudged Emily, half hug, half push. "Sweetheart, it's time to pull out all the stops and find out who is your stalker and what, exactly, they want before something worse happens and someone gets hurt."

She despised him—and rightly so. Mac called himself seven kinds of fool all the way home. He hadn't meant to spill his guts the way he had. It went to show how sex could mess with a guy's brain. That had to be it. He'd been feeling all warm and cuddly and even thought he and Emily might have started something worth preserving—and not just for the sake of his relationship with his son.

Stupid, stupid, stupid.

He wouldn't be surprised if she didn't try to run. Hell, he wouldn't blame her if she did.

Hating like hell the way he was shaking, he put in a call to Renee. "I need to talk to you. I haven't been entirely honest...."

"Yes, I know," she said, her voice steely and decidedly unfriendly. "I've got Emily Gilley and Ed and Jayne Cooper here in my office."

His stomach clenched. "They're already there?" That had been fast. He could scarcely wrap his mind around the events of the past few days. Everything had begun to run together. Once, everything had seemed so clear-cut. Now, he no longer knew what he wanted.

"Yes," Renee answered, "and you'd better come in right now. Emily is very upset. Understandably so. We have quite a bit to talk about, don't you think?"

Inhaling deeply, he knew she was right. After all,

he wasn't the only one with secrets that needed to be revealed.

"I'm on my way," he said, concluding the call. He'd put his truth out in the open, and now the time had come for Emily Gilley to do the same.

Inside Renee's office, Emily felt torn. While Renee spoke to him on the phone, she paced. "I'm not sure I'm up to seeing Mac. Not right now," she protested, wishing she didn't feel as if her heart had splintered in half. "Not yet. Not after what he did."

"You have to, sweetheart," Jayne murmured, grabbing her and putting her arm around Emily's shoulders. "This is a neutral place. It's all for the better."

Pretending she didn't see the long look that passed between Ed and Jayne and Renee, Emily took a deep, shuddering breath. "Let me go check on Ryan."

"He's fine," Renee put in. "Eva and Charlie are watching TV in the break room with him. I've got one of my assistants in there keeping an eye on all of them."

Emily nodded, aware of both anticipation and dread. When Mac had told her who he was and what he believed to be the truth, again she'd had to fight not to react on impulse. Trying to stand still, to deal with this latest crisis was a new form of torture, especially when every protective mothering instinct she had screamed at her to grab her son and run—fast and far. She knew she could disappear in another state, another small town. After all, she'd done it once before.

But eventually, as it always did, her past would catch up with her. In this instance, she knew Mac would not rest until he found her again. And she couldn't blame him.

Because, whether she agreed with him or not, he truly believed Ryan was his son.

"Do you think he is?" Renee asked bluntly, almost as if she'd read Emily's mind. "Ryan's father, that is."

"I have no way of knowing." Emily paused to catch her breath, her misgivings threatening to turn into full-blown panic. "I know nothing of my son's history or parentage. I've always understood that the adoption was arranged through a private broker my former husband contacted."

Renee waited, apparently aware Emily hadn't finished speaking.

"There's also Desiree and Franco." Emily inhaled. "For the longest time, I've believed that my husband fathered Ryan with one of his mistresses. I've suspected she is my stalker—Ryan's biological mother."

"Desiree?" Renee watched her with a keenly observant gaze. "In other words, you think your former husband is Ryan's true father."

"Yes."

"That all makes sense, too," Jayne breathed. "And the mistress could have resented giving up her son, so she's the one threatening you."

Emily nodded. "Even though this all happened in New York, I think she might have followed me here to Texas to try and get Ryan back. Though why she won't admit it is beyond me. She keeps talking about some jewelry."

"Maybe she plans to blackmail you," Jayne put in. "Have you considered that?"

"That's another possibility," Renee agreed.

"I hadn't thought of that." Emily closed her eyes. "And here I was actually feeling sorry for her, thinking she might have been forced to give up her baby. If she's planning to try blackmail, she'll soon figure out that I have nothing. You can't get blood from a stone, so if that's the case, she's way off base."

"Then Mac comes along and says he's the father." Renee's lips thinned. "What a nightmare."

Relieved that someone actually understood, Emily spoke with quiet, worried firmness. "Yes. Mac's story came out of nowhere."

Jayne rubbed the top of her back, no doubt trying to console her. Knowing if this continued, she might choke up—or worse, dissolve in tears—Emily moved away. She gave her friend an apologetic look as she went to stand as far away from the door as possible. There wasn't room to pace or she would have done that instead.

Clearly not understanding, Jayne moved also, taking a place at Emily's side. At the move, Emily felt a rush of gratitude. She'd never had a friend like Jayne, someone willing to have your back no matter what.

Just as Emily was attempting to compose a way to tell Jayne how much that meant to her, Renee stood. "Why don't you and I go have a chat with Desiree? Just the two of us."

Once again feeling a discomforting sense of finality, Emily found herself nodding. She stepped away from Jayne, her head held high. "Lead the way."

Following Renee down the long hallway to the back part of the sheriff's department, Emily mentally rehearsed what she wanted to say to the woman who might or might not be the mother of her son.

"I think you might have a private word with Franco, too," Renee said, her tone conversational. Something about the too-casual sound of it made Emily stop and look at her.

"Just me?"

With a shrug, Renee flashed a rueful grin. "Both Desiree and Franco have hired lawyers. They won't even say boo to me. But maybe they'll be different with you."

Though her heart had started pounding and her mouth had gone dry, Emily nodded. "If one of them is responsible for making my life a living hell, then I'd like to know."

"Good girl." Renee's grin widened as she patted Emily's shoulder. "Here we are."

As they paused at the metal door, Emily caught herself wishing that Mac was by her side, which surprised her. She supposed she'd need time to get used to the idea that he had become her enemy.

"This is where we're holding Desiree," Renee said as she unlocked the door.

"I'm not sure I want to be alone with her," Emily admitted.

"Oh, you won't be. I'll be standing right by the door watching, though I won't participate in any discussion you two might have. All right?"

Since she didn't appear to have a choice, Emily nodded.

Desiree looked up as they stepped inside, her hostile expression not boding well for the chance of any meaningful conversation.

"Emily wants to have a word with you," Renee announced.

"I have nothing to say to either of you." Desiree sneered, her gaze sweeping over Emily disparagingly before returning to Renee. "Leave me alone."

Though Renee's jaw tightened, she didn't respond.

Taking a deep breath, Emily stepped into the room. A small holding cell, the room had the basic necessities—a cot, a chair, a sink and in the corner a toilet with a plastic shower curtain that could be pulled around for privacy.

Perched on the edge of the cot, with her extensive makeup still intact, Desiree wore the petulant and wounded look of a martyr. "My lawyer says I'll be out of here as soon as court opens up Monday morning. So go away, and quit bothering me."

Ignoring her, Emily took another step closer. "I want to talk to you about my son."

Desiree's perfectly shaped brows rose. "You have a kid? Carlos never mentioned that to me."

Stunned, Emily stared. "How long were you two together?"

Waving a languid hand, her scarlet nails flashing, Desiree smiled. "Two years," she said proudly. "He'd just left my apartment the day he was murdered."

Though this statement probably should have bothered Emily, she'd long ago come to terms with Carlos's multiple infidelities. Briefly she wondered if Desiree knew she'd been one in a long parade of others, then decided nothing would be gained by mentioning that.

"You don't know about my son?" Emily asked softly, not sure whether to believe her.

Emphatically, Desiree shook her head. "I don't like kids. Why do you care what I think about your son anyway?"

"No reason." Glancing back at Renee, who stood with arms folded near the exit, Emily dipped her chin to indicate that she'd finished.

"You're really stupid," Desiree said as Emily prepared to leave the room. "And I know you have my jewelry. I'm not leaving until I get it back."

Turning, Emily met the other woman's gaze straight

on. "I don't have any jewelry. Everything was sold to pay off Carlos's debts."

Desiree narrowed her eyes. "You sold my necklace? That was my price for giving Carlos the ultimate gift."

"Ultimate gift?" Emily froze. "What exactly did you give him?"

But Desiree's expression had shut down. "None of your business. Leave me alone."

Once out in the hallway, Emily exchanged a look with Renee. "I don't know what to think about her."

"I think she's telling the truth." Renee frowned. "She doesn't know anything about Ryan."

"Maybe not, but what ultimate gift did she give Carlos? Do you think she could have given up her baby?"

Renee eyed her for a moment before slowly nodding her head. "I suppose it's possible, but what matters to us right now is if she did she doesn't want him back, I don't think she's your stalker."

Emily wanted to protest but didn't. Renee wouldn't understand why she still wanted to know if Desiree was Ryan's birth mother. Then again, maybe she would. After all, if that was the case, Mac's claim to fatherhood was completely misguided.

Oddly, this thought didn't make her feel any better.

"Are you okay?" Renee asked, concern plain in her eyes.

Emily nodded. "Let's go talk to Franco."

This time, when she stepped into the small room, after a quick, rage-filled glance, Franco refused to even look at her. Every attempt at conversation was met with "talk to my lawyer."

After the fifth response, Emily shrugged and motioned to Renee that she was ready to go.

As they were walking back to Renee's office, Mac arrived. He strode through the front door, his powerful, well-muscled body moving with easy grace. His closed-off expression gave nothing away. Emily glanced at him, trying like hell to study him dispassionately and wishing her heart still didn't skip a beat when she looked at him.

The same hopeless attraction flared—even now that she knew he was her enemy.

Seeing them, he stopped, indicating with a sweep of his hand that they should precede him. As they filed into Renee's small office, everyone in the room stared at him, including Emily.

Devilishly handsome, the air of isolation around his tall figure might have been only her imagination—or not, considering the hostility with which everyone in the room regarded him.

Those piercing sapphire eyes locked on her. "Emily." She noted he kept his hands at his sides, clenched into fists. Who was he angry with—her or himself? Why did she even care?

For the space of a heartbeat, she stared back at him, struggling to find the right words. It turned out there were none.

He measured her, his look cool and appraising. She studied him back, unable to keep from drinking up his powerful male beauty with her eyes. As if he knew, for an instant his impossibly blue gaze sharpened. Her traitorous pulse quickened in an involuntary response.

She should have hated him for what he'd done to her, the way he'd made her have hope and desire again when she thought she never would. But as a mother, she could understand the depth of the love that drove him—love for a child he'd never known. If Ryan really was his, how could she even think to take his son away from him now?

Yet how could she bear to give up her baby?

"I'm sorry," he said, his words meant only for her, his expression grim. She shriveled inside at his words, aware she could not accept his apology. How could she, when she didn't even understand why he bothered to make it?

"I trusted you." Her voice broke. Even worse, she knew he could read the hurt and accusation in her eyes. More than anything, she wished she could turn her heart cold, change it to stone, so this raw, primitive grief wouldn't overwhelm her.

Once again, as though she sensed Emily's inner agony, Jayne put her arm around her shoulders, pulling her close and giving Mac her best back-off-from-my-best-friend glare. Emily loved her for that.

Clearing his throat, Ed shuffled his feet awkwardly, clearly wishing he was somewhere else, anywhere else.

"Emily? Are you all right?" Renee stood like a weary Amazon, her desk her shield, looking from Emily's little group to the man standing alone near the doorway, his handsome face a dark mask.

With her throat closed up, Emily could only nod, which apparently was enough.

"All right, then. Why don't we start with you?" Renee said to Mac, before including the others in her sweeping gaze. "I think we all have a right to know the truth. Are you the one who's been terrorizing Emily here?"

Mac blinked, his mask slipping for a moment to reveal shock. "I... No. I have no idea who that is."

"Obviously, this person believes he or she's the boy's natural parent," Renee continued. "I've talked to Joe, and he admits that neither of you have found any conclusive evidence proving that you're the father, either."

At that, Emily felt the weight on her chest lighten somewhat.

"Why don't you tell me—us—what exactly are your reasons for believing Ryan is your son?" Renee asked.

Mac shifted his weight, hesitating as he measured her for a moment before inclining his head. He watched Emily, clearing speaking directly to her. "As you know now, your husband was under investigation. The Feds were watching him. NYPD was helping. They asked my partner, Joe, to be a part of that investigation. He's a whiz at anything electronics related, one of the best in the country. He was on loan from the Albany P.D."

"So?" Crossing her arms, Renee regarded him the way she might regard a hostile witness. "What has all that to do with any of this? Get to the point."

Mac met her gaze, unblinking. "I will. Joe was there when my wife died. Hell, he helped pull her out of the wrecked car. He was at the hospital when my son was born."

One corner of his mouth twisting upward in a grimace, he continued, his voice bleak with sorrow. "Joe also was there in Manhattan, watching via hidden cameras, the day your adopted son appeared—exactly one day after my own baby was stolen."

Emily's heart dropped into her stomach. She could only imagine how he must have felt. Somehow, from somewhere, she found her voice. "While I'm sorry for your loss, you still haven't given me a valid reason to believe that my son was—is—your missing baby."

Pinning her with his gaze, a swift shadow crossed his face. "Joe recognized him. When he saw Ryan, he called me immediately, though doing so was against protocol. He swore the kid was a dead ringer for my missing son."

Emily felt as if ice had crept into her every pore. Swaying, she closed her eyes for a moment, trying to gather her composure. Her sorrow and worry and fear had become a huge, painful knot in her heart.

"Why didn't you simply ask me back then?" Emily whispered. "I'm sure Carlos and I could have cleared things up immediately."

One muscle worked in his jaw, as if he held his emotions in check. "Because I couldn't. Due to the nature of his investigation and how close they were to an arrest, I had to wait until the Feds made their move. The night before the sting was supposed to go down, Carlos was murdered."

Closing her eyes, Emily struggled to swallow past the ache in her throat. She knew the rest. "And I disappeared," she whispered.

"Exactly."

They all went silent for a moment, digesting this.

"What about the pictures of Ryan in the hospital nursery that Emily got from the stalker?" Renee eyed him like a hawk. "Have you ever seen them before?"

"No," he admitted. "Though they could have been any infant in any hospital. The little knitted cap on the baby's head looked familiar."

"A lot of hospitals use those for preemies," Jayne retorted. "That doesn't mean anything."

"You're right. It doesn't. That's why I'd like a DNA test to solve this once and for all."

"Once you were able to seek out Emily, did you contact the authorities to help you look for her?" Renee asked, her voice still brusque.

Now Mac looked down. "No, we did not."

"Why not?" Her glance clearly said she thought he'd been foolish. "You were a cop. You know we help our own. I'm sure the Albany P.D., hell, the NYPD would have pulled out all the stops to help you."

Jaw clenched, he shook his head. "First off, we had no proof. Second, Joe went out on a limb for me. Telling me could have jeopardized the investigation. I couldn't risk it."

"So Emily vanished with the baby you believed was yours. And you had no idea where she'd gone?" Renee asked, her tone sympathetic.

"Right. No idea whatsoever." He shrugged his shoulders. "It took me four and a half years to track her down."

Shocked, Emily met Renee's eyes before slanting a look at him. "You were stalking me."

"Not like that," he said, his dark gaze full of pain and regret. "I swear to you that wasn't me."

Before Emily could respond, Renee held up a hand.

"You moved here because she lived here?" she asked, narrowing her eyes at him.

He didn't look at Emily when he answered. "Yes."

"And befriended her and got her to trust you," Jayne put in, the accusation in her voice mimicking the way Emily felt.

Mac didn't answer. He didn't have to—his actions spoke for themselves.

"Was your coming to work for the sheriff's department part of this plan, too?" Renee asked, her vexation evident in the lines that creased her brow.

"No, that simply happened. Circumstances. Maybe. What does any of this matter now? Look." Including them all in his gaze, he gestured. "Despite what you all think of me, I didn't intend for anyone to get hurt. I have been searching for my son for five years. I don't expect any of you to understand that, but finding him was—is—the only thing that made life worth living."

Watching him, Emily empathized. She should hate this man, not sympathize with him. Yet who was she to say she would have done things any differently had their situations been reversed?

She might not be Ryan's birth mother but he was the son of her heart—and would always be, no matter what the outcome of all this…no matter who had biological rights.

Blinking, she realized someone must have asked her a question.

"Emily," Jayne prodded. "Do you want to press charges?"

"For what?" Dragging her hand across her eyes, Emily pushed away her exhaustion, focusing on the fear. Fear would keep her sharp, help her make sure she didn't make any mistakes that could potentially endanger her son. "Though he's been dishonest, Mac hasn't committed a crime."

Jayne looked at Renee, who slowly nodded. "She's right. As a matter of fact, I'm going to recommend that we shelve this topic for now and focus on catching this wacko who's been tormenting our Emily."

"I'd like to continue to help," Mac put in, startling Emily, and from the look on Renee's, Jayne's and Ed's faces, them all.

Then, as Emily opened her mouth to protest, he held up a hand. "Hear me out. Who better to protect Ryan than someone who cares about him? I can promise you I'd give my life for him. You can't ask for much more than that."

This time, rather than keeping his emotions locked

inside, he let her hear the anguish in his deep voice, see the torment in his eyes. Guilt and anger and fear and…all the same emotions she had tumbling inside her. They shared this, if nothing else.

Actually trembling, a tear slipped silently down her cheek as she watched him, aching.

Renee glanced from one to the other. "I'll leave that up to Emily. Honey, what do you want to do?"

Emily slowly nodded. "I'd like him to help."

"All right." Renee turned to face Mac. "I'm going to let you stay on the payroll but only because we need to catch this stalker. That is your only duty, understand?"

"I understand," he said. "I want that stalker caught as badly as anyone here."

"I doubt that," Emily said, before she thought better of it. "Thank you," she told Renee, turning away from Mac, unable to keep looking at him. "I'll be going now."

Then, giving Jayne's arm a squeeze in gratitude and nodding at Ed, she went to collect her son and head on home before she shattered into a thousand pieces.

Chapter 11

Mac watched her go. The instant she'd disappeared from view, everyone turned to stare at him: Jayne, as if he was something distasteful she'd found under a rock; Ed with curiosity; and Renee with a drained sort of compassion.

"What the hell were you thinking, Riordan?" Renee asked. "Do you have any clue?"

He gave her a rueful smile. "Not really," he admitted. "I'm sure that must be really apparent to the rest of you."

"It's okay, man." Ed came forward, earning a death glare from his wife. "I would have done the same thing if someone had stolen Eva or Charlie."

Despite her obvious desire to side with her friend, even Jayne had to nod in agreement. Regardless of that, she stepped forward, poking him in the chest, her gaze shooting daggers at him.

"Don't you hurt Emily," she said, drawing out the words so he'd understand they were important. "I don't care what you feel you have to do. I even understand some of it. But Emily loves her boy, and he loves her. She'd do anything for him. Get that? Don't you do anything to mess that up."

"I won't," he promised, realizing he meant it. "I'm going to catch this stalker. You wait and see. Once I do, then we'll find out the truth about Ryan's parentage."

"But—" Jayne began, until Ed squeezed her shoulder in warning.

"A man has a right to know the truth about his son," Ed growled. "Don't begrudge him that."

Ridiculously grateful, Mac tried to summon up a smile. When he couldn't even manage that, he nodded, knowing the other man would understand.

As he turned to go, his cell phone rang. Joe's number showed on the caller ID. Immensely grateful that his friend—rather through some sort of cosmic connection or mere coincidence—had chosen to call just when Mac needed him most, he answered.

"What's up?" Joe asked, his cheerful voice somehow easing a bit of the knot in Mac's chest.

As he hurried outside, Mac filled his best friend in.

"You need me?" Joe asked, the seriousness in his tone telling Mac he only needed to say the word.

"I'm okay." Even though he wasn't.

"Listen, I have some vacation time coming. I'll book a plane ticket and head on down there," Joe said, as though he knew everything Mac hadn't put into words.

"I don't know...." The protest was only a token, and both of them knew it.

"I'll call you with my flight information," Joe said firmly. "You can pick me up at the airport."

Capitulating, Mac ended the call. He should have talked to Joe sooner. Now that he had, he felt better than he had in days. Having someone on his side—not just anyone but a savvy criminal investigator—would definitely go a long way toward helping him learn the identity of Emily's stalker.

Driving home, listening as Ryan chatted happily in the backseat, Emily felt utterly and completely depleted. As though by his actions, Mac had stripped all the vitality out of her, laying her inner soul bare and exposed to the unfriendly elements. She'd come to think of him as a friend. No, she'd come to think of him as more than that....

Ruthlessly, she cut off the thought. It was too dangerous and completely and utterly foolish. But Mac was right about one thing. If she was going to protect Ryan, she had to find out the truth about his parentage.

Was he Mac's son? Or, as she'd long suspected, Carlos's with one of his mistresses? After all, Carlos had always claimed that Emily had been the reason they couldn't have a child of their own, even though neither of them had ever been tested. His refusal to allow not only tests but also in vitro fertilization told her she would never have the child she craved. She'd labeled herself barren, in her darkest moments, when she'd despaired of ever having the children she craved. Adoption had been the only option Carlos would consider.

And then Ryan had come along, like the brightest, shiniest gift, the greatest blessing Carlos could have given her. Her son was her world, the family she'd never had, her heart. She could no more lose him than she could live without breathing.

Could she risk this? How could she not?

Reluctantly, she faced the fact that the time had come for her to know the truth. First up was to find the stalker, which, since no one appeared to be having any luck, she'd have to do on her own.

She had a plan. Despite Desiree's denial, Emily was willing to bet Carlos's old mistress was the stalker, which meant if she'd been the one to birth Ryan, Mac had the wrong baby. And since Desiree must have signed away her rights—no doubt in exchange for cash—she wouldn't have as much of a chance of gaining full custody. That was assuming the documents could be found. No doubt they were among the boxes of paperwork the FBI had seized after Carlos's death.

That was it. Emily actually smiled to herself the first time all day. If she could get Desiree to admit to being the stalker, she could take the first step to end this craziness once and for all. The DNA test would just be icing on the cake. Her life would go back to normal, and her future with Ryan would be safe and secure.

Her plan had only one flaw: Desiree's repeated denial. What did the other woman hope to gain? And where did Franco come in on all of this? His arrival—with Desiree—was too much of a coincidence. That meant the two of them were concocting some sort of plan.

What a mess. Briefly, she closed her eyes, wondering what had happened to her cherished dreams of a life in a clapboard house with a white-picket fence, playing in the sprinklers on a warm summer day.

Now she was embroiled up to her elbows with two people—one known and the other not—who believed themselves to be Ryan's rightful parent.

The truth of it was—no matter the biology or

genes—she was Ryan's mother. And if she had any say in things, no one could ever take that away from them.

Glancing at her watch, aware her rather shaky plan hinged on the hope that the stalker would call her personally this time, she began to mentally rehearse exactly what she would say. And she still had to decide if she should let Mac in on her plan.

Sunday passed in a blur of indecision. Mac must have picked up the phone to call Emily at least half a dozen times, always reconsidering. Joe's flight would be in around nine that evening, so until then, he was just killing time.

He puttered around the house, restless as a caged lion but unwilling to go into town and risk running into Emily or any of her friends.

Finally, Mac made the two-hour drive to the airport. He parked outside in the arrival area of Terminal C and waited.

When Joe finally emerged, striding across the pavement, several women did double takes, making Mac grin. "New haircut?" he asked, as Joe pulled open the passenger door and, after tossing his carry-on in the backseat, climbed inside.

"Yep." Joe grinned back, shaking Mac's hand. "Ladies seem to like it." Shrugging, he settled back. "Tell me everything."

So Mac did, starting at the beginning. Joe listened without interruption. With every word, Mac felt more and more at ease, as if unburdening himself to his best friend had removed a huge pile of rocks from his chest.

When Mac wound down, finishing with his declaration to Emily and the meeting at the sheriff's department, Joe winced. "Ouch," he said. "Maybe not the best move."

Concentrating on driving, Mac glanced at Joe and grimaced. "I know, but I couldn't keep lying to her."

"You have *feelings* for her?" Joe sounded incredulous. "We're talking about Carlos Cavell's widow? The woman who stole your son?"

"We don't know that," Mac protested, aware that by doing so he was answering in the affirmative.

"We don't?"

"We're not a hundred percent certain."

"Mac!" Joe leaned forward, peering up at Mac like he was afraid his best friend had lost his mind.

"Well, it's true," Mac continued. "I've asked for a DNA test. Until we do that and I get the results back, there's no way we can be—"

"Take me to meet him," Joe interrupted. "I'll bet I'd know after one look at him."

Mac glanced sideways. "Just like that, huh? You're serious?"

"Yes."

Mulling this over, Mac finally shook his head. "Things are too volatile right now. You'll eventually meet him, I promise."

"It's your call," Joe said. "You know who else I want to hang out with? Renee. I haven't seen her in ages."

Mac nodded. "We're nearly there. If it's okay with you, we'll grab a beer and then make tonight an early one. It's been a long day."

"Sure, no problem," Joe said easily. "I'm going to be here a week. There's plenty of time to get everything done."

The next morning, Mac got up and, after he and Joe killed a pot of coffee and demolished six fried eggs, drove his friend over to Emily's house. They stopped at a doughnut shop along the way and picked up a dozen assorted as a sort of peace offering.

"Are you sure she won't mind?" Joe asked, for what had to be the third or fourth time.

"Reasonably," Mac answered. "Though she has to be at work by nine, if we time this right, it'll work out. Even if she won't spend much time with us, at least you'll get to see Ryan."

"Fantastic." Joe stretched and yawned. "I called Renee while you were in the shower. She and I are having lunch later."

Mac nodded, already thinking about Emily. As they pulled up in her driveway and his heart began to pound, he told himself it didn't matter if she rejected him. If she didn't want to let him in, he'd hand her the doughnuts and go on about his business.

Joe got out with him, one hand on Mac's shoulder in a show of support as Mac rang the bell.

A moment later, Emily answered the door, looking both frazzled and beautiful. Her short, spiky hair was messier than usual, reminding him of the way she'd looked after they'd made love. His body stirred, though he immediately clamped down on that chain of thought.

Next to him, Joe made a sound of approval low in his throat.

"What do you want?" Her gaze locked on his before she deliberately let it slide away to inspect Joe.

"Truce?" He held out the box of doughnuts.

Staring at him, unsmiling, she shook her head. "No, thanks. I'm not interested."

Joe stepped forward, his brilliant smile in place. "Hi. I'm Joe Stalling, Mac's friend from Albany." He held out his hand.

Taking it, Emily briskly and efficiently dispatched with pleasantries. "Nice to meet you," she said, before turning back to Mac. "After all this, you think you can show up on my doorstep with a box of doughnuts and expect me to forgive you?"

He winced, aware of Joe watching silently. "I'd really like to talk."

"It's Monday, and I have to get Ryan to school." Pointedly, she glanced at her watch. "We're already running late."

"How about after?" Though he hated begging, he supposed he deserved this for what he'd done to her.

Stepping back, she attempted to close the door on him. "I have to go to work."

"Remember I'm still working your case," he reminded her, grateful when she paused. "Joe has years of experience working in New York. He's kindly offered his assistance."

This, more than anything else, got her attention.

Finally, she nodded. Leaving the door open, she stepped back, motioning for them to come inside.

"Wait here," she ordered, turning her back on him and disappearing into the hallway.

Standing in the small tile square that marked her foyer, he gazed out at the colorful living room of the house that had once felt like home. The aroma of fresh coffee filled the air, and he could hear the sounds of Emily helping Ryan get ready for school.

Mac felt a longing so sharp it was painful, well aware that he might have once stood a chance of being part of this…if only he'd kept his mouth shut…if he'd been willing to build a life based on a lie.

"Pretty nice," Joe commented, looking around. When Mac didn't respond, he slugged his arm. "And now that I've seen her, I can understand how you two got involved."

Throat aching, Mac could only nod.

A moment later, Emily returned, a freshly scrubbed and grumbling Ryan at her side. Next to him, Mac felt Joe instantly go on full alert.

"Hey, Mac!" Ryan grinned, sauntering over toward Mac and holding up his hand for a fist bump. Smiling, Mac bumped him back.

"I brought doughnuts," he said, holding up the box and drawing Ryan's gaze back to him from Joe.

"Ryan already ate breakfast," Emily put in, her pinched voice matching the flatness in her eyes.

"Please, Mom? Can I have just one?" Ryan pleaded, alternating jumping up and down and shooting covetous looks at the doughnut box.

Mac wanted to side with Ryan but, afraid if he did so he'd have the opposite effect, said nothing.

"Please, please, please?" Ryan kept on. "Just one teeny chocolate glazed doughnut? Pleeeeeease?"

Finally, with a small smile at her son, Emily gave in. "Just one," she said, ruffling his head. "And you'll have to eat it on the way to school."

Crouching down, Mac lowered the box to Ryan's level, letting him open it. "Choose whichever one you like."

The boy didn't even hesitate. "That one," he said, snagging a chocolate-topped doughnut. Mac handed him a napkin, unable to tear his eyes away as Ryan bit in with obvious delight.

"Hi, there," Joe ventured when no one made a move to introduce him to the child. Like Mac, he crouched down, putting himself at the same height as Ryan. "I'm Joe, Mac's friend."

"Hi." Barely glancing at him, Ryan focused all his attention on his sugary treat.

"I've got to take Ryan to school," Emily said, eyeing Mac and then Joe from under her long lashes. "Do you want to wait outside in your car? I should be back in five minutes or so."

Careful not to show how hurt he was that she rightly no longer trusted him enough to let him wait in her living room while she was gone, he nodded. "Sure."

As he trudged to his patrol car with Joe and the rest of the doughnuts, he couldn't help but wonder if she meant to return. He couldn't blame her if she went on to other things and left him sitting alone in her driveway.

"Ryan doesn't look at all like I expected," Joe said thoughtfully once they were safely inside the patrol car. He flashed Mac a halfhearted smile. "Though I swear I can see Sarah in him."

Mac felt too queasy to smile back. He opened his glove box and removed the DNA test kit he'd brought. "I was going to give her this, but now I don't know if it's a good idea."

Frowning, Joe looked from the book to him. "You gotta do what you gotta do."

And that, for Mac, pretty much summed everything up in one neat sentence. Still, that didn't mean he had to like it.

He and Joe waited silently, each lost in their own thoughts.

Seven minutes later, Emily pulled in alongside them. He started to get out of his car, but she motioned him back.

"We can talk right here," she said, lifting her chin.

"In the car?" he asked, stung yet again. "I'd really like a little privacy."

Wearing the pained expression of a martyr, she made a show of checking her watch before reaching for the back car door handle. "You're the one who brought a friend."

Point taken.

Getting in, she dipped her chin in a nod at Joe, then returned her attention to Mac, eyeing him like a fly trapped in a web watching a spider.

Mac eyed Joe, considered asking him to leave, then thought better of it. He noticed his friend watching Emily in the rearview mirror rather than turning around to face her.

"What do you want?" she finally asked.

Taking a deep breath, he leaned over the console and placed the doughnut box next to her on the backseat. "As I've said, I'd like a DNA test." He crossed his arms. Despite the pain and contempt he saw flash in her eyes, he held his ground. "That's the only way we'll know for certain."

"And then what?" Despite the slight tremor in her voice, she held her head high. "If he is your son, are you planning to sue for custody? You have to know I'll fight you with everything I have."

He dipped his head, not sure how to answer. He owed her the unvarnished truth, but he was no longer one hundred percent confident he knew what the truth was.

"I don't know," he finally told her. "Let's deal with that bridge when we cross it."

"I see." The bitterness in her tone told him she didn't really. "I'll go by the drugstore and pick up a DNA test kit."

"No need. I already have one." Heart hammering in his chest, he held it out. He'd ordered it first thing after arriving in Anniversary. "I'm going to use the same lab the sheriff's department uses. Renee said we can get faster results that way."

Instead of taking it, she crossed her arms. "I don't have to do this, you know. I can make you get a lawyer, and we can go to court. I can delay this for months, maybe even years."

At her words, Joe tensed but said nothing. Mac could tell from his friend's profile that Joe wanted to jump into the conversation in Mac's defense. While he appreciated that, Mac was glad he didn't.

Aching, Mac regarded Emily. "Yes, you could do that. But I have to think you'd want to know the truth, too. For yourself and for Ryan."

She opened her mouth and then closed it.

"Not to mention getting rid of the stalker. If it turns out Ryan is my son, this other person will have no claim on him."

As his words registered, she swallowed hard. Finally, mouth twisting, she took the proffered box. He couldn't help but notice how her hands trembled as his did. "You might not be his father, you know."

"I know," he said, though he didn't believe that for an instant. "Your stalker and your former husband could be the birth parents."

At his ready agreement, she stiffened. "Yes. Or there's a third possibility. Neither of you could be a genetic match. Ryan could be exactly as he was presented to me—a baby whose mother gave him up for adoption—someone completely unknown."

Joe quietly snorted. They both ignored him.

"Anything's possible," Mac finally said.

Emily stared at him. The hope she couldn't hide, along with the stark pain in her beautiful eyes, nearly undid him. "I never meant for this to happen," he muttered, trying to pretend Joe wasn't eavesdropping on the entire conversation. "You, me, none of that."

"Really?" Again she crossed her arms, shooting several glances at Joe, as though wishing he'd give them some privacy and leave. "What did you mean to happen exactly? You came into our lives, ostensibly to help find my stalker, comforted me, pretended to care about me…"

Her voice broke, and she turned away to stare out the window. The way she hunched her shoulders told him how hard she tried to hold on to what had to be the shattered remnants of her self-control.

More than anything, he wanted to take her arms. It was part of his penance that he couldn't.

Half of him wanted to ask for the DNA test kit back, to tell her never mind and ask if they could simply go back to the way they'd been before. He'd seen a glimpse of the possible future, a future so full of hope and love and happiness that he'd scarcely dared to believe it. But he'd known then as he did now that if they were going to try and forge such a potential life they could have no lies in between them. Ah, but that didn't make him want it any less.

Still, he knew that no matter the outcome he had a right to know the truth. *They* had a right to know. *Ryan* had a right to know, too. Even Emily had to see that.

He hadn't meant to hurt her. Clearly, he had hurt them both. Hell, if she felt one tenth as bad as he did, it's a wonder she could even look at him.

The future he'd begun to envision had also vanished, like wisps of smoke in a gale force wind.

"I'm not going to leave Anniversary, you know," he finally said. "No matter what happens."

At these words, she turned to face him, every angle

of her body speaking defiance. "I don't care what you do."

They both knew this was a lie.

When he didn't immediately respond, she nodded. Then, clutching the DNA test kit, she climbed out of his car and went back to her house, her back ramrod straight and her gait stiff. Unlocking her front door, she slipped inside, never once looking back.

Mac shot Joe a warning look, letting him know he'd better not say a word. Then he started the car and drove off.

Once inside, Emily crumbled. Tossing the stupid DNA test kit as far as she could, she stomped into her kitchen, pouring herself a big mug of her own coffee, dumping his down the drain. She'd be damned if she'd drink his.

Before she'd realized it, half an hour had passed. Almost out the door, her house phone rang.

Caller ID read *Unknown Caller*. Maybe…heart suddenly pounding, she answered.

"I'm glad I caught you before you left for your job," the metallic voice said. Due to the amount of distortion, she couldn't make out whether the caller was male or female. It sounded like a sexless computer android.

"I'm not playing your game." Emily kept her voice even. "I'm sick and tired of you hounding me."

"Tough," the computer-generated voice sneered.

Ignoring this, Emily continued. "If you really feel that Ryan is your child, why the secrecy? Don't worry, I know Carlos had a mistress. He had more than one, so if this is Desiree, you'll still have some proving to do. Come forward. Let's meet and see if we can hash this out."

The silence on the other end of the phone line told her she'd succeeded in startling her caller.

"You lie," the person said.

"No, I don't." Keeping her tone light, Emily sighed. "It seems Ryan is a popular child. I've already got one person claiming to be his father who has asked for a DNA test. What's one more? Why not add your name to the mix?"

Again the caller went quiet. When he or she spoke again, the androidlike tone sounded thick and even more unsteady. "Are you serious?"

"Dead serious," Emily answered, then winced at her unfortunate choice of words. "Either put up or shut up."

"Stupid woman. I'll meet you. At your place. Look for me, because I won't be calling to let you know when to expect me." There was a click, and Emily knew her stalker had hung up. Whether it was Desiree, Franco or a complete stranger, Emily knew she'd finally set things in motion toward a conclusion.

Placing the phone back in the cradle, she realized she was shaking. Suddenly, she didn't want to be alone in her house any longer. She snatched her purse off the counter, hurried to her car and went in to work.

Luckily, the vet clinic was busy all day and time flew by. She skipped her daily run, vaguely afraid to go near the park, and grabbed a quick sandwich from the deli down the street. She ate at her desk, explaining she had a lot of paperwork to catch up on due to her absences.

Whenever the image of Mac came to mind, she ruthlessly pushed the thoughts away. But as the day wore on, she found herself wondering if she should tell him that she'd spoken with her stalker. Someone needed to know what she'd done. Since Mac had a vested interest in catching this person, too, filling him in would be a smart idea.

So what if the idea of seeing him again had her stomach tied in knots?

She waited until thirty minutes before closing time to call his cell phone. He answered on the second ring, the deep timbre of his voice sending a jolt into her heart.

Though she knew she could simply tell him what she'd done over the phone, she suddenly wanted to see him in person.

"We need to talk," she said.

"Name the time and the place and I'll be there." The hopeful huskiness in the statement made her regret her impulsive decision.

She couldn't back out gracefully—not now. "Come over around seven. That'll give me time to fix Ryan dinner."

"I can come earlier and bring something. Chicken, pizza, burgers you name it."

Wearily, she closed her eyes. "No, thank you. I need to talk to you while Ryan is occupied. His favorite television show comes on at seven. He won't be listening in if we talk in the kitchen."

After the vet clinic closed, Emily picked Ryan up at the day care and went home. She cooked Ryan's favorite hamburger-and-macaroni dish, and they ate together. Despite the ball of worries lodged in her stomach like lead, she choked some down and managed to smile and nod as Ryan recounted his day at both kindergarten and day care.

Dinner finished, Ryan went to take his bath before his show came on, and she washed the dishes. Every sound, from a particularly insistent blue jay outside to Ryan turning off the faucet, had her jumping. If real life were like the campy horror movies she used to watch when she was younger, the stalker would be jumping out of her closet at any moment.

Luckily, that didn't happen.

Trying to laugh at her fears, as it grew closer to seven, she couldn't keep herself from checking out her reflection in the mirror. After brushing and then spiking up her hair, she smoothed a little lip balm over her lips and waited for the doorbell to chime. She refused to pace or give in to the temptation to keep taking peeks out the window.

Despite her halfhearted attempts to act normal, she didn't fool her son.

"Mom?" Ryan asked, emerging from the bathroom already in his pajamas, his dark hair still damp. She breathed in the clean scent of Ivory soap and hugged him tight, only releasing him when he protested.

"What's up, kiddo?" she asked.

"Is someone coming over?"

Since he didn't know anything about what had happened, she nodded. "Mac is, sweetheart. How did you know?"

He grinned. "You're still wearing your work clothes and makeup, Mom." Lifting his small hand for a fist bump, he crowed in triumph, making her smile. "Normally, you change."

"You're right. I guess I can't put anything past you, huh? Your show's about to come on, so you'd better turn the TV on."

The words had barely left her mouth when the doorbell chimed, instantly sending her heart into overdrive.

"That's him! That's him!" Ryan yelled, running toward the door.

"Wait!" she shouted, going after him, reminding him

she needed to look through the peephole, but she was a few seconds too late.

Not knowing who was on the other side, he yanked the door open just as she reached him.

Chapter 12

Luckily, Mac stood on her doorstep rather than the stalker. After shooting Mac a stay-put glare, Emily turned the same look on Ryan. Upset and furious, she grabbed her son and moved him back. "How many times have I told you we don't open the door without checking to see who's out there?"

His blue eyes widened at both her tone and her actions. "But you said Mac was coming over. I knew it was him ringing the doorbell."

"That doesn't matter," she chided, still shaking from the burst of adrenaline. "That could have been anyone. We have to be careful. You know that."

For a second, Ryan looked like he wanted to argue. Then, apparently thinking better of that, he hung his head, his lower lip wobbling. "I'm sorry, Mommy."

She hugged him close and breathed a kiss on his forehead. "Okay. But promise me you'll remember next time, okay?"

"Okay." Sniffling, he raised his head. Then he grinned, eyeing the paper bag Mac held. "Whatcha got?"

"Ryan!" About to apologize, she closed her mouth as Mac crouched down, holding the bag out toward Ryan.

"Why don't you look and see?" Mac said.

Reaching for the bag, her son had the presence of mind to glance at her for permission. She yanked her gaze away from Mac's and slowly nodded, giving her permission.

With that, Ryan snatched it and yanked it open. "Cookies!" he breathed. "Oh, Mom. Can I?"

"May I," she corrected automatically. Though she limited sweets, occasionally she let Ryan indulge. "Yes, you may."

"Can—may I have a glass of milk to go with them?"

Though she kept a pleasant expression on her face, she felt awkward, dealing with her son in front of the man who might be his biological father. Still, she kept her voice neutral and consoled herself with the knowledge that her son didn't suspect anything was amiss. "Of course, if you promise to use the coaster on the coffee table. I'll bring it to you in a minute."

"Thank you so much!" Impulsively, Ryan gave Mac a quick hug, then tore off to the living room to plunk down in front of the television just as the opening credits started for his show.

Still feeling self-conscious, she avoided meeting Mac's gaze. "He'll be busy for the next half hour. Come on into the kitchen."

As she led the way, she could feel his eyes burning into her back. She had to fight an overwhelming—and completely stupid—need to turn and walk into his arms and let him hold her. Instead, she busied herself pouring Ryan's milk, feeling the heat of Mac's gaze as she carried it out to her son.

When she returned, she flashed him a halfhearted smile and pulled out her chair at the kitchen table, motioning for him to do the same. She tried not to watch as he settled his large body, dwarfing the ordinary chair.

To give him credit, he didn't try to rush her. Instead, he simply placed his tanned hands on top of the table and waited.

"Where's your buddy?" she asked, stalling despite her resolve.

"He and Renee went out," he said, unsmiling. "They're old friends who go way back."

Swallowing, she nodded. For her part, she took an inordinate amount of time getting settled, unable to keep from fidgeting. This felt more uncomfortable than she'd thought it would.

Finally, once she was seated, she squared her shoulders and looked directly at him, surprised at how painful that was. "I asked you to come over because I got a call from the stalker today."

A sharp intake of breath as he leaned forward was his only reaction. Pretending his nearness didn't affect her, she relayed the conversation, tumbling her words over each other in an effort to get them all out.

When she'd finished, Mac sat back, jaw clenched. "Are you sure that was wise?" Emotion deepened his sapphire eyes, changing them to midnight. "What if this person—let's say you're right and she actually is one of your former husband's mistresses—has grown more unstable? What if she's dangerous? You know she said you would pay."

"I've always known she's unstable." Agitated, as much by how badly she wanted to touch him as she was by the situation, she jumped from her chair and began to pace. "Why the hell else do you think she'd be breaking into my house and calling me?"

A muscle worked in his jaw. "You do realize you are putting yourself in danger?"

Swallowing hard, she boldly met his gaze. "It's time to end this, once and for all. I'm counting on you to keep me safe."

Though he didn't react verbally to her words, something smoldered in the depths of his eyes.

"Do you think you can do that?" she pressed.

"I can," he promised, his voice husky. "You can count on that."

"Thank you." Now that the hard part was over, she exhaled and pulled a chair out to take a seat before reconsidering. "Would you like something to drink? I have cola, iced tea, lemonade or water."

"Water is fine, thanks."

After she'd placed their glasses on the table, she again took her seat, gripping her glass with both her hands.

His bare arm, tanned and muscular and silky with hair, rested on top of the table. She fought the urge to touch him, to stroke his skin and see the desire blaze into life in his eyes. Even now, when she knew he'd used her, she still ached for him. How foolish was that?

"All right, let's get what details we can. Are you reasonably certain the caller was female?" He sounded exactly like the cop he was—professional and detached... too detached. Though no doubt his calm, reassuring tone was meant to soothe, conversely she wanted to shake him up, ruffle his feathers, make him show emotion—any emotion.

In the other room, Ryan laughed out loud at his television show, a reassuringly normal sound that was so out of place with this discussion that she jumped.

What the hell was wrong with her? She took a deep breath. "No. I'm not certain at all. There was no way to tell. As you know, whoever it was uses some kind of computer-generated voice software."

"But they agreed to meet you. Did they say where?"

Aware he wasn't going to like this, she took another deep breath, wincing. "Here. Whoever it is plans to come here. And he or she said they'd show up unannounced."

He reached across the table and captured one of her hands in his big one, startling her. "I don't like this," he said.

"Of course you don't." Though she didn't pull away, she couldn't resist a verbal jab. "After all, someone else actually might have a valid claim to what you think is yours."

This time, when pain flashed across his rugged face, she steeled herself and didn't break their locked gaze.

He leaned forward, toward her rather than recoiling away as she would have expected, keeping her hand trapped in his. He looked big and powerful, and she knew a second's fleeting longing that he would always be there to protect her and keep her safe and warm.

This proved that fools never, ever changed.

About to open her mouth and ask him to leave now that their business had been concluded, a slight hesitation in his expression made her wait.

"Listen, I've been thinking about this. About him." Speaking quietly, he glanced back toward the living room, where Ryan sat still engrossed in his program, eating his cookies and drinking his milk. "I wanted you to know that I'm not going to try and take him away from you."

"What?" She blinked, blank, amazed and disoriented. "Say that again?"

"If the DNA test proves I'm—" he lowered his voice again "—if it proves I'm his father, I'm not planning to try and sue for custody."

All she could do was stare and then stupidly ask him why not.

"You're his mother now." He gave her a long look, full of rueful warmth. "I wouldn't take that away from him, away from either of you. But I would like to work out some sort of visitation agreement with you. So I can be in his life, help him grow up. And assist you if you need me."

Shock siphoned the blood from her face. Dizzy, for a moment she thought she might actually faint. Shaken and momentarily speechless, she found herself gripping his hand so hard the tanned skin turned white.

She stared at him, her heart pounding. "Are you…" The words caught in her throat. Swallowing hard, she tried again. "Do you really mean that?"

"Of course I do. If Ryan is my son, I have a right to share in his life but not to ruin it. He loves you, and I can see how much you love him."

Almost afraid to believe it, she focused on her breathing—in and out, trying to center herself, attempting to accept his words as truth. This felt like a miracle, as if her prayers had not only been heard but answered.

Eyeing him across the table, his generous mouth quirked in the beginning of a smile, she couldn't catch her breath. With her throat aching and tears pricking the back of her eyes, she wasn't sure she could speak.

What a wonderful, amazing man.

Again, she longed to go to him and wrap her arms around him. Instead, she pushed past the emotion clogging her voice. "Thank you," she said, the warmth in her voice warring with the huskiness of raw emotion. "I can't tell you how much that means to me."

Now he did smile, dazzling her. "I'm not your enemy, Emily. I never was."

In the other room, the familiar jangle of a popular commercial came on. Ryan appeared, carrying the wadded up cookie bag and his empty milk glass. He froze when he saw his mother's tear-filled eyes and devastated expression.

"Mommy? Are you all right?"

"Of course I am!" Pushing herself up, she took his glass from him, carrying it to the sink and rinsing it out. The very ordinariness of the action helped calm her. "Throw your empty bag in the trash," she told him, glad she sounded relatively normal again.

Once he'd done that, she crouched down and opened her arms wide. "Come here, you."

He ran over, gave her a quick hug and then began squirming when she tried to keep him close. "Mommmmy! My show's coming back on."

As soon as she let him go, he rushed back into the other room.

"See what I mean?" Mac's eyes were suspiciously bright. Seeing that, she gave in to impulse and went to him, hugging him from behind. The instant her arms wrapped around his shoulders, he froze, as if her touch was too much for him to handle just then.

She felt foolish, immediately backing off, though she refused to apologize. If anyone deserved a hug, Mac did.

A moment later, he uncoiled himself from his chair.

"I'd better be going. Before I do, I'll call Renee and make sure she's arranged for twenty-four-hour surveillance."

Biting her lip, she hesitated. After all that he'd given her that night, she knew she owed him this much. She decided she'd go for it and say exactly what was in her heart. "I thought this was your case."

In the middle of paging through the contact list on his phone, he paused. "This is," he said slowly, a question in his eyes.

"Then wouldn't you be the one doing surveillance?"

"We take shifts. I'm not sure who's on tonight."

"I asked you to come over." She took a deep breath, then plunged on before she thought better of it. "Why don't you just stay here? I have a foldout couch in my office. You can sleep there."

Staring at her, when he finally offered her a slow, arresting smile, she knew he'd accept her offer.

"Let me run to my house and throw a few things into a bag. I'll be back in less than an hour," he said, his deep voice vibrating with emotion.

Throat tight, she followed him to the door, watching as he got into his car and drove off. Then she secured the dead bolt and the other lock, hoping her stalker didn't decide to make an appearance in Mac's absence.

As he drove away, Mac finally admitted to himself the truth. He loved her—with every beat of his heart and more. He loved her. And he could never let her know. He wondered if fate would ever stop laughing at him.

He'd found his son, true. But he'd also found the woman with whom he wanted to spend the rest of his life.

Allowing himself a moment to dream, he pictured them: he and Emily and Ryan together. A family.

But now she'd never believe he wanted her for herself. She'd always believe he only said he loved her because of the child they shared. Sadly, he couldn't blame her. So he'd best learn how to be grateful for what he could have.

At least he'd once had a family—unlike Joe, who'd never married. That's why Mac had been glad to see the spark of interest between Joe and Renee.

The knowledge that his friend might finally have something going on in the romance department made Mac happy. Joe had always been the perpetual bachelor, dating a large variety of girls but never getting serious. He'd even refused to bring a date when he'd gone out with Mac and Sarah, claiming being a single third wheel was better than introducing his best friends to women he didn't love.

Though Mac had found this slightly odd, Sarah always seemed to find it amusing. Good-naturedly, Mac had humored them both.

As he thought of this, he was struck by something else. Remembering those days no longer felt as painful. He hummed under his breath and realized this was because not only had he finally located his son but he'd found a woman with whom he wanted to spend the rest of his life.

He merely had to stop an overzealous stalker and then spend all his time showing her that they were meant to be together.

Throwing a couple of clothing changes into a gym bag, he grabbed the essential toiletries. He tossed the bag in his car, checked his mailbox and his answering machine, then climbed into the car and headed back toward Emily's.

As he pulled out of his driveway, his cell phone rang. It was Joe.

"What's up?" Mac asked good-naturedly.

"I need a favor." Joe sounded distracted, almost upset. "I ran out of gas in my rental car and need you to bring me five gallons. I'm stuck in the middle of nowhere." He rattled off a location clear on the opposite end of town.

Glancing at his watch, Mac knew he didn't have time. "I'm going to call one of the other deputies to meet you. I have somewhere I really have to be."

"Come on, Mac," Joe groaned. "I have a huge flower arrangement in my car, along with a giant stuffed toy bear. Since they're for Renee, I really don't want anyone else in the department to see them. Imagine the ribbing she'd get. Please come yourself. It will only take a few minutes. I promise."

Again Mac checked his watch. It had only taken him twenty minutes to get home and pack. Running out to rescue Joe would take at least that long. He didn't want to leave Emily alone in case the stalker chose that night to pay her a visit.

"I'll do what I can," Mac finally told Joe. "Rescue will arrive in a few minutes."

Aware Mac would be back soon, Emily tidied up while letting herself imagine various scenarios, all of them erotic. She couldn't imagine what had possessed her to invite the man to stay overnight in her home, but now she was glad she had. Though she knew it would be difficult to resist temptation. Did she even want to resist? That was the million-dollar question.

She sighed. Despite his enigmatic exterior, she sensed his inner vulnerability, especially concerning her son. Rather than pushing her away, his Achilles' heel pleased her and made her desire him even more.

But she would have to table her wants and needs right now. They had more important issues to worry about.

Once she'd finished straightening up the house, she sent Ryan to brush his teeth and pulled out the sofa bed. She found sheets in the linen closet and made the bed up for him, imagining Mac's tan skin against the smooth sheets. Smiling at the image, she finished making the area as comfortable as she could.

When the doorbell chimed a scant thirty minutes later, Emily wiped suddenly sweaty hands down the front of her jeans and grinned. That had been really quick. She'd just gotten Ryan tucked into bed.

After unlocking her dead bolt, she opened the door, her welcoming smile fading as she belatedly realized she should have followed her own rule and used the peephole.

It wasn't Mac standing on the doorstep. It was Mac's friend, dressed in a hoodie and jeans. This time, she got a good look at his blond hair, tanned skin and blue eyes—the same color as Mac's.

"Can I help you?" she managed to ask politely, though before she finished speaking she already knew. Heart pounding, she tried to close the door, but he stuck his foot inside and gave it a heave, sending her stumbling back against the wall. He pushed his way in, kicking the door shut behind him.

"I've come to get Ryan," he said, his tone coolly menacing as he pulled out a pistol and pointed it at her. "Bring him to me. Now."

Emily stared, even as panic coiled in the pit of her stomach. She didn't know what to say, how to choose the right words—something that wouldn't set him off. She had to do something to buy her a little time until Mac returned. Because there was no way in hell she was letting this man take her son.

When she didn't respond, the man took a step closer, a shadow of annoyance darkening his face. "I mean it. Get the boy. Now."

Instead of moving, she studied him. His compact medium build spoke of latent strength, and he walked with a fighter's muscular stance.

Either way, his presence here didn't compute. Though he appeared extremely dangerous, he couldn't be her stalker. After all, Albany, New York, was a long way from Texas, and he'd just gotten into town.

So what did he want with her son?

Either way, she'd die before she'd let him take Ryan.

"Did you understand me?" The silken voice he used to ask the question made her even more ill at ease. "I'm not asking again. Get Ryan."

"What do you want with my son?" she demanded, refusing to let him see how much he frightened her.

"*Your* son?" His laugh came rimmed with icicles. "Do you mean the baby you had stolen from the hospital nursery so you could adopt him?"

She felt as if her breath had been cut off as she glanced uneasily over her shoulder. "If this is some misguided attempt to help Mac, you need to stop. He wouldn't want this. He and I are already working something out. I know you're his best friend, but this is completely unnecessary."

At her words, he gave her a black, layered look. "You honestly think—"

Before he could finish, the doorbell rang. Mac? Her heart leapt into her throat as she instinctively turned toward it.

"Don't move," Joe barked. Keeping the gun trained on her, he crossed to the door and checked the peephole. "Perfect," he said, unlocking the dead bolt. "Reinforcements."

Franco and Desiree stepped inside. Desiree's overly made-up eyes widened at the sight of the gun. Franco, on the other hand, appeared unfazed. He faced Joe and cocked his head. "Did you find the diamonds?" he asked.

"Not yet," Joe answered. "I'm sure it's here somewhere. Right, Emily?"

Afraid to move, she slowly shook her head. "I'm sorry, but like I told Desiree earlier, all of the jewelry was sold."

"And that's why we're going to grab the kid," Franco sneered. "Because I'll bet you find the diamonds real quick if you're worried about your son."

Emily froze. "That's why you want Ryan?" she asked softly, watching both Franco and Joe. "Because of some stupid, nonexistent diamonds?"

Joe started to speak, but Franco cut him off. "Half a million of ice isn't stupid. Now go find the jewelry or we're taking your kid."

Terror skittered a path up her spine, giving her an involuntary shiver. "Please," she appealed to Joe. "You're Mac's friend. You have to know he believes Ryan is his son. Don't do this."

Joe laughed, a bitter sound. "I know what he believes. He's always believed that. But I know better. Ryan isn't his son. He's mine."

"Yours?" she repeated. Was that madness glittering

in his eyes or certainty? Either way, she knew she stood on dangerous, unstable ground.

She needed to buy enough time for Mac to return. Mac was her only hope.

"Please." She kept her tone cordial, like that of a hostess speaking to a welcomed guest. "I'm confused. Mac told me the exact same story, except he said Ryan is *his* son. He can't be both."

He stared hard at her, his mouth twisting. She looked back as calmly as she could, hoping he couldn't see the wild tattoo of her rapidly beating heart.

Finally he looked away, appearing to be considering her words. Though judging from the tight grimness of his jaw, she didn't have long before he lashed out again.

Inwardly shuddering, she prayed she could pull this off. Time…she needed time. And she needed Mac. She could only hope he returned soon.

As he considered her words, his handsome face twisted in rage, a caricature of the icily composed man who'd faced her a moment ago.

"Sit down." Motioning with the gun toward her sofa, he waited.

She sat.

"Let me tell you about me and Mac." He sneered the words. "We've been best friends since we were in the third grade. We competed for everything, too. Sometimes I won. Sometimes he won. Neither of us really minded—until Sarah came along."

"Mac's wife?"

"That's right. She and Mac started dating, and then they married. I tried, but I couldn't let her go. All along, I was the proverbial third wheel. Mac used to tease me because I never brought dates around them."

The way he looked at her, as though she was supposed to comment, had her scrambling for something noncommittal to say. "You sound like you all were a close group of friends."

A muscle worked in his jaw, making her think she must have made a mistake. But then he slowly nodded. "We were. Until Sarah realized I loved her and began to love me back."

Mac sighed. Though he'd debated honoring Joe's request, he couldn't risk leaving Emily alone much longer—not with the stalker about to show up at any moment. Luckily, he'd called Ed, and he'd agreed to go help Joe. Now Mac was on his way to Emily's. He'd already been gone longer than he deemed feasible.

Pushing the accelerator to the floor, he sped toward Emily's house, praying he wasn't too late.

He got there in less than ten minutes, noting the unfamiliar car parked in her driveway. The maroon sedan looked vaguely familiar, despite its spectacular ordinariness.

He parked in front of a house two doors over. He approached on foot, with his service pistol drawn.

Instead of going to the front door, he ran to the side. Keeping close to the building, he rushed around to the back. Of course, being prudent and careful, Emily had locked the door. However, he was willing to bet she was like thousands of other people and kept a spare key stashed somewhere nearby.

He found it inside a fake rock she'd evidently purchased for that purpose. Quietly, he unlocked the back door and slipped inside.

From the other room, he could hear voices. A man stood with his back to him, and it appeared Emily was seated on the couch.

Not taking the time to consider, he rushed across the kitchen into the den, weapon raised.

"Sheriff's department. Hands where I can see them," he ordered, adrenaline pumping so hard it took him a second to recognize the man with a gun pointed at Emily.

"Joe?" Despite his shocked disbelief, Mac kept his best friend in his sights. "I thought you'd run out of gas on the other side of town."

Joe's mouth twisted. "I thought you would be on your way to help me."

Mac frowned. "I sent Ed. What the hell is going on?"

Before he'd finished speaking, Franco rushed out of the bedroom, gun drawn. "Drop it, cop."

"Or I shoot Emily," Joe said.

Because he had no choice, Mac dropped his gun.

Moving quickly, Joe kicked it aside.

"I found it!" a familiar feminine voice trilled. Desiree tripped into the living room, grinning. She held a battered cigar box in her hands. "It was in the kid's room, in a toy box, under a bunch of stuffed animals. He never even woke up."

"Open it," Franco commanded, keeping his weapon trained on Mac.

Slowly, she did, licking her brightly painted lips as she displayed the stunning diamond jewelry inside. "There's even more," she breathed. "I'll bet there's a million bucks worth of stuff in here. Maybe more."

"Perfect." Franco smiled back. "Now we'll be leaving. Go, honey. Go."

Desiree headed toward the door, Franco right behind her, gun still drawn. "Are you coming, Joe?"

Joe shook his head. "Hold on," he barked. "We're not done here. I want the kid."

Mouth open, Franco stared. "Why? We've got what we want. Let's go."

"No," Joe snarled, his gaze flicking from Emily to Mac and back to Franco. "We're not leaving until I get what I want. I need you to back me up. I came here for Ryan. I want my son."

"Your son?" Both Mac and Franco spoke at the same time. Mac kept his gaze trained on Joe, who had his pistol pointed at Emily. Franco still stood near the doorway next to Desiree, weapon raised.

Joe's expression of fury warred with the sadness in his blue eyes as he nodded. "I know you thought he was yours. But he's not. He's mine. Sarah was going to tell you—actually, we both were going to tell you that night at dinner. But then she had the accident and…"

Mac could only stare. "Are you insane? Sarah wouldn't have cheated on me. And not with you. You were—are—like a brother to me. To both of us."

Joe laughed. And then Mac knew.

A tumble of confused images ran through his mind. None of them made sense. "How could you? You're my best friend. I trusted you like a brother."

For an instant, regret darkened Joe's chiseled features. "I'm sorry. We never meant for anything to happen. But we grew so close…."

Keeping his eyes trained on the man he'd believed was his best friend, Mac tried to understand. Inside, something clicked, an answer finally sliding into place.

Instead of anger or grief, he felt only…bitterness. He would have thought learning such an awful truth about his wife and the man he'd called his friend would rip his heart out. But in the past five years, he'd done a lot of questioning. In hindsight, a lot of things about his marriage hadn't added up.

And now Mac had to face the fact that the baby he'd believed to be his might in reality be Joe's.

That hurt more than he would have believed possible. "Mac," Joe said, "you've got to understand. Sarah and I truly loved each other. She was going to ask you for a divorce so we could marry and raise our child together."

Our child... The baby Mac had always believed was his.

Now Joe's beyond-the-pale assistance in the search for Ryan all made sense.

Even so, it took every ounce of willpower Mac possessed to keep from staggering under the impact of Joe's words. Now that they'd been spoken, looking back, he wondered how he hadn't seen something, guessed anything. Had he really been so blind?

"You had no reason to doubt her," Emily said, almost as if she read his mind. "Or him."

Mac kept his gaze trained on Joe. "Now I understand why you were so fanatical about locating the baby. You kept on even when every lead seemed to be a dead end. But not because you were so desperately trying to help a man who'd lost everything. You did it because you had a vested interest."

"I lost everything, too," Joe cried, pain flashing in his blue eyes.

"Maybe you have, but that doesn't explain how we've ended up with this. Both of us armed and against each other."

Franco cleared his throat, drawing their attention.

"Look," he said, reaching for the front door. "This is all very touching and all that, but I got what I came for."

Brandishing the cigar box like a weapon, Desiree grinned. "Me, too. Looks like sending you all those letters finally paid off."

"Letters?" Emily asked. "Those were from you?"

"Yep," Desiree said proudly. "You took what was mine. I wanted it back. Now, I've got it. I hope it works out for you with all this." She gestured at Joe and Mac. "But Franco and me, we gotta run."

"Don't move," Joe ordered. Then, when Franco ignored him, Joe shot him in the back.

Chapter 13

Emily gasped as Franco fell, a bloodstain spreading over his upper shoulder.

"You shot him." Desiree's voice echoed Emily's disbelief. "Oh. My. God."

Blue eyes narrowed, Joe looked from Desiree to Mac to Emily. "So what? Consider this proof that I'll do what I have to do to take back what's mine."

Sobbing, Desiree sank to the floor alongside Franco, still clutching the all-but-forgotten cigar box.

Heart pounding, Emily flinched as Joe took a step toward her. She prayed the loud gunshot hadn't awakened Ryan.

"Go get the boy," Joe ordered again, this time through clenched teeth.

Emily shook her head, breathing in quick, shallow gasps. "No."

"Put the gun down," Mac ordered. "Come on, Joe. There's no way you'll get away with this. It's over."

Joe didn't move, the barrel of his gun never wavering from Emily. "It's not over. Either I get my son or I'll shoot Emily."

"That makes no sense," Mac growled.

Joe glared at him. "It makes just as much sense as what you did. You befriended her, all so you could take what you thought was yours. We're not so different, you and I. I want what's mine."

Shaking his head, Mac took a step closer to Joe. "Without a DNA test, we have no way to know for sure that you're the father."

Afraid to breathe, Emily watched as Joe eyed Mac.

Then, apparently seeing a hint of uncertainty in Joe's expression, Mac kept talking. "Sarah and I were still intimate right up until she died," he said. "I could just as easily be Ryan's biological father as you."

Face mottling with rage, Joe's jaw worked. "You're lying," he sputtered, waving the gun in the air between Emily and Mac. "Sarah told me she wasn't—"

Behind Joe, Desiree slowly got to her feet. Mascara had made black streaks run down her cheeks. Moving slowly, she raised the cigar box and slammed it in the back of Joe's head.

Joe staggered, clearly stunned.

"Get down!" Mac dove for him. Out of reflex, Joe squeezed off a shot. It went into the roof above Emily's head, sending plaster raining down on her.

Elbow to the throat, Mac knocked the pistol away from Joe. Emily scrambled to retrieve it. Desiree stood nearby, shaking.

Mac grimly cuffed his best friend and began reading him his rights. "You have the right to remain silent—"

"Mom?" Ryan said, sleepy-eyed and standing in the doorway closest to Joe. "What's going on?"

Emily's heart stuttered. "Ryan, go back to your room," she told him, breathless and shaky but stern. "I'll be in there in a minute. I promise."

To her relief, the little boy turned immediately and disappeared around the corner.

"Wait up, Ryan." Handcuffed and subdued, Joe stared in the direction the boy had gone. "Please, let me see him. Just once more."

"No." Emily lifted her chin and glared at him. "If you'd gone about this in a different way, I might have considered it. But you've not only endangered me but him. You have no rights, as far as I'm concerned."

Then she looked at Mac, shaking with the after-effects of shock and a sudden, furious rage. "Do I need to call 911?"

"I can call it in," he said quietly. "Go tend to Ryan."

"What about Franco?" a clearly shaken Desiree asked. "We need an ambulance. He's still alive."

"We'll get him some help," Mac promised. "Please, sit down before you fall and hurt yourself."

Though she nodded, Desiree sank to the ground alongside Franco, who still hadn't moved. Emily noticed the other woman continued to cradle her box of precious jewels as though they were a lifeline. Personally, she was surprised that Desiree hadn't fled when she had the opportunity. She must really have cared for Franco.

Shaking her head, Emily hurried out of the room. The last thing she heard was Mac calling dispatch.

When she reached Ryan's room, her little boy launched himself at her. She held him and attempted to calm him. Though half-asleep, he'd seen the strange man and the guns. She'd explained things simply, by saying Joe had been a bad man and since Mac was a policeman he'd arrested him. Luckily, Ryan didn't appear to have seen Franco lying on the floor.

Downplaying any danger, including the gunshot that had awakened him, she smoothed his dark hair away from his perfect little face and kissed his forehead.

"Do you think you can try and go back to sleep?" she murmured. "It's a school day tomorrow, and I know you don't want to miss kindergarten."

He clung tightly to her and shook his head violently. "That man was going to shoot you, wasn't he?"

"It's all right, sweetheart. Mac saved us."

Her little boy raised his head and met her gaze, looking much older than his five years. "I want to tell him thank you," he said.

"You can, later. I promise." She kissed him again, love making her chest tight. "He has to get that man to jail and then there's paperwork and all kinds of boring stuff. You can thank him in the morning."

Rather than arguing, he nodded, eyes already half closing. She continued to hold him, rocking softly and murmuring in a soothing voice.

When his even breathing revealed he'd fallen back asleep, she eased her arms out from under him. Once his head was on the pillow, she covered him and got up. About to leave, she stopped, unable to keep from standing near the side of his bed and gazing down at him with her heart full of wonder and love.

He was her baby…her son. No matter what the DNA

test proved, nothing would ever change the relationship she had with him.

She closed Ryan's door behind her and prayed the wail of the approaching sirens didn't awaken him again. She went to rejoin Mac and Desiree.

Later that night, after the ambulance had taken Franco to the hospital, Emily answered a barrage of questions. Renee handled the investigation herself, despite her bandages and the obvious pain her shoulder wound caused her. Desiree had to hand over the jewels and was arrested on charges of breaking and entering. She was bundled into the sheriff's car, along with Joe, who faced a barrage of charges.

Mac insisted on escorting Joe downtown himself. He left without even a backward glance at Emily. She supposed he was still stunned over Joe's revelations. She couldn't help but wonder what kind of woman Mac's wife had been to have an affair with her husband's best friend.

Though Mac had clearly not believed her when she said she hadn't known about the diamonds, she'd only told the truth. The one area she'd never thought to search was her son's toy box.

Wandering into the kitchen, she poured a glass of white wine and drifted back into the living room. More than exhausted, she felt drained. As she collapsed on the sofa, she knew her life was about to change. She couldn't put it off, couldn't run and hide. She had to face her future—Ryan's future—straight on, with her head held high.

After all, she'd done nothing wrong and everything right.

Sipping her wine, she reflected on Mac's promise

not to take her son away if he was the father. With those words, he'd managed to erase all the shadows over her heart.

Except what would happen if Joe was Ryan's biological father, rather than Mac? She supposed it wouldn't matter now. It looked like Joe would be going away to prison for a long, long time.

She carried her half-finished glass to the sink, rinsed it out and went to bed. Everything could be dealt with in the morning. What she needed now was sleep.

Once all the necessary paperwork had been completed and with Joe and Desiree safely in custody and Franco recuperating in the hospital, Mac finally headed home as dawn began to lighten the eastern horizon.

Joe's revelations had stunned him. But now, while he hated learning he'd been played for a fool by his wife and his best friend, he'd found a sort of acceptance. All that was ancient history and completely insignificant compared to what really mattered to him now.

All that mattered was Emily and Ryan…Ryan and Emily. When he crawled into bed as the sun came up, their names were the last two things on his mind.

Later that morning, a ringing telephone jarred him out of a deep, dreamless sleep. Instantly alert, he answered.

"Did I wake you?" Emily asked, her husky voice sending a thunderbolt of desire straight through his groin.

"I'm okay," he managed to say, rubbing his eyes and squinting at the clock, trying to read the time. "How about you?"

"Last night was tough, but it's a new day."

"And Ryan?" he asked.

"Ryan was a little upset last night, but this morning he seems fine. I just dropped him off at school." She took a deep breath. "I was wondering if you had a few minutes to talk."

He couldn't squelch the warm glow that spread through him. "Would you like to have breakfast?"

"Thanks, but I've already had it several hours ago." A thread of nervous determination ran through her voice. "Could you meet me at the sheriff's department in, say, thirty minutes?"

He frowned but kept his tone light. "Sure. Would you mind telling me why?"

"I'd rather not. See you there." She disconnected the call.

Now what? Refusing to speculate, he took a quick shower, towel dried his hair and got dressed. Since it was nearly one, he skipped his normal coffee and snagged a stale, leftover doughnut on the way out.

Driving the speed limit, he arrived at the same time as Emily. He turned in just as she pulled up into the parking lot.

Though she had to have noticed his car, she continued on inside without even glancing at him, her back ramrod straight.

A kernel of worry lodged in his stomach. What was going on? He parked and went inside.

Emily waited for him inside Renee's office. He raised a brow at her as he walked in. "What's up?" he asked.

She motioned to a box in the middle of Renee's desk—the DNA kit. "We need your sample. I've already gotten Ryan's, and Renee is going to get Joe's."

Renee handed him a swab. "Go ahead and swab the inside of your cheek and place that inside this bag."

Again he looked at Emily, but she wouldn't meet his gaze. He did as Renee had requested. When he'd finished, he turned the bag around but didn't hand it to Renee—not yet.

"Are you sure you want to go through with this?" He laid a gentle hand on Emily's arm. "You don't have to, you know."

"Yes, I do." Though she met his gaze bravely and spoke in a calm voice, he could see the worry in her caramel eyes. "You were right, what you said before. I have to know the truth. And Ryan should know who his father is."

He nodded, feeling a sense of finality as he accepted her decision. His life—everything leading up to this point—clicked into place as he handed the sealed bag to Renee. Unable to resist, he glanced at Emily, only to find she was intently watching Renee.

"I'll hand carry this to the lab we use for crime scenes," Renee said. "They're in Dallas, and they promised to get the results as quickly as possible. We'll include not only yours and Joe's samples but one from Carlos, as well," Renee told them.

Emily started at that. "How is that possible? Carlos has been dead five years."

"NYPD has some on file. I pulled a few strings, and I'll need you to sign some forms. Since Carlos's widow is the one requesting it, I'm confident they'll meet our request. We should know in three days tops," Renee said.

"Will you inform Joe of the results?" Mac asked,

keeping his voice steady. "Even though it's likely he'll be transferred to the county jail?"

"Of course. I can visit him there." A shadow crossed Renee's face. "I have to say that I was surprised. I had no idea he was involved in any of this."

"Me, either," Mac said grimly.

"You lost a friend."

"No, I learned the man I'd thought of as a brother was a backstabbing, wife-stealing liar." Aware of the bleakness of his tone, Mac looked away, lost in thought.

He couldn't help but wonder if he'd really known Sarah at all. She'd been nearly full-term when she'd lost her life in that accident, all the while maintaining that she and Mac were the parents. He wondered how long she would have kept up the farce. Had she truly known which man actually was the baby's father, or had she only suspected? That was one question to which he'd never know the answer.

As Mac turned to go, Emily voiced what they both feared. "What if Ryan really is Joe's son?"

Renee shrugged, looking at Mac.

He squeezed Emily's shoulder, glad of an excuse to touch her. "We'll deal with that when we come to it."

Though she nodded, he could tell from her downcast eyes and closed off expression that the idea troubled her greatly.

It worried him, too. But he refused to let the outcome of the DNA test affect the plans he'd made for the rest of his life—plans that, no matter what, included Emily and Ryan.

The next three days passed in a blur. Emily kept busy. In fact, Jayne and Tina told her she seemed positively driven. She worked hard, kept busy and managed to avoid Mac, though doing so was easy since he appeared to be also avoiding her. She couldn't exactly blame him. Still…

She didn't know what she would do if the DNA test revealed that Joe was Ryan's father. She prayed it would be Mac. Thinking how things had changed almost made her smile. A few days ago, she would never have believed she'd be hoping Mac would have a connection to her son.

Her doorbell chimed, making her jump. As if her thoughts had summoned him, Mac stood on the front porch, wearing his uniform and looking impossibly handsome.

Glad Ryan was still at school, her traitorous heart skipped a beat at the sight of him. Even now, even after knowing he'd played on her attraction to him and used her to get closer to Ryan, she still wanted him.

Schooling her expression into a bland, pleasant look, she opened the door. "Hey."

His gaze raked over her, sending an involuntary shiver down her spine. "Do you have a minute?"

Slowly, she nodded, struck dumb by the power of her own foolish need. Blood humming in her ears, she stepped aside, indicating he could follow.

As he moved past her so she could close the door behind him, she couldn't help flashing back to when she'd been locked in his embrace. She shook her head to dispel the disturbingly carnal images. Even now she wished things had been different.

She'd actually allowed herself to believe in a future. That was progress, was it not? Progress. Right…when she couldn't even perceive of a future without him. It was more of a step back than anything else.

She loved him. The power of that knowledge made her wince. She couldn't let him know. To protect herself, she knew she'd need to call on any shred of latent acting ability she might have in order to talk to him as if what he'd done, what they'd shared, hadn't mattered.

"What's up?" she asked Mac, perching on the edge of the couch as though she didn't have a care in the world. Her voice sounded serene and steady, even though her insides were quaking.

"I came to apologize," he told her, a ghost of a smile flitting across his handsome features. "I know to you it seemed like I tried to get close to you because of Ryan, and maybe in the beginning, that's all it was. But something changed."

Keeping an iron grip on her emotions, she waved his words away. "No worries," she said brightly. "I don't have any hard feelings against you."

His expression darkened. "You might be listening, but you're not hearing what I'm trying to tell you. This is important, Emily. To both of us."

"To both of us?" she echoed, surprised by the flash of anger she felt. Suddenly, she'd had enough of pretending. "Is it? So I'm supposed to sit here and let you say whatever you feel you have to in order to salve your conscience?"

Shaking his head, his brittle smile softened. "That's not why I'm here. Yes, you deserve an apology—actually, you deserve so much more."

Inwardly, she cringed. "I don't—"

"Let me finish." He came closer, stopping within touching distance. "Something started between us…

something with potential. I didn't intend for that to happen, but—"

Horrified, she cut him off. "I don't want your pity."

"This is not about pity," he growled, grabbing her and pulling her into the crush of his embrace. Stunned by the instant desire warring with fury, she stiffened rather than struggled, fighting against her instinctive response.

"Let me go," she said, barely getting the words out before he covered her mouth with his own.

Her resolve shattered with his kiss. Hunger, passion and more blazed to life, and she clung to him, dizzy and trembling and full of need.

When he finally raised his mouth from hers, his impossibly blue eyes blazing, she couldn't make herself pull away. There was an implicit claim in his embrace. daring her to deny what had sparked to life.

"This," he said quietly, nose to nose. "We have the potential of something special between us. You see it. I know you do. No matter what happens with the DNA test."

She couldn't answer, couldn't allow herself to hope, couldn't even begin to find the words. Forcing herself to look away from him so he wouldn't see the truth in her gaze, a movement out the front window caught her eye.

"Look," she gasped, moving away to stare at the sheriff's cruiser pulling into her drive.

"Renee." He sounded as worried as she. "The DNA test results must have come back already."

Heart racing, Emily nodded. As she moved toward the door, he touched her shoulder, stopping her.

"Promise me you'll think about it," he said, letting her see the hope that shone fierce from his blue eyes.

Giving the barest of nods, she answered. They went to the door together, standing side by side, arms touching.

Renee glanced from one to the other but didn't speak as she held out the results.

Emily accepted the tan envelope from the other woman, amazed that her fingers didn't shake.

Again, Renee's sharp gaze swept from Mac to Emily and back again. "Is everything okay?"

Numb, Emily nodded. Mac did the same.

"Then, I'll leave you two alone," Renee said, turning and marching down the sidewalk. She got back into her car and drove off.

Once her car had disappeared from view, Mac took Emily's left hand and led her inside. Fingers still locked with hers, he closed the door and locked it. Though she wanted to let herself relax into his touch, she couldn't.

Jittery, jumpy, she fingered the envelope, wondering why she felt so reluctant to finally learn the truth.

As if he sensed this, he squeezed her hand, his fingers gentle and warm. "Do you mind waiting to open it? I'd like to settle things between us first."

Hesitating, fighting the urge to let herself lean into him for comfort, she decided to go ahead and speak the truth. "I'm not sure we have anything to settle."

"But we do." He took a deep breath, studying her intently. "I want you to know this. If Joe is the biological father, I'll help you fight any attempt he might make to gain custody."

At first she couldn't quite process his words. When she finally did, she supposed they made a twisted kind of sense. "Why? Because you want to get him back for sleeping with your wife?"

"No." He dragged his hand through his hair. "For the same reason as before when I told you if I was the father, I wouldn't try to take your son from you. Because I want what's best for Ryan. Staying with you would be the best for him."

Staring at him, she saw the truth of his words in his face. "You honestly mean that, don't you?" she asked with a dawning sense of wonder. "No matter what the outcome of the DNA test, you truly care about my son."

"And about you," he put in quietly. "I know it's early and we're barely getting to know each other, but there's something there. Tell me you feel it, too."

The tenderness in his gaze made her knees weak. Tongue-tied and feeling warm, she couldn't speak so she nodded instead.

"This is your choice," he continued, the intensity in his voice telling her he meant what he said. "If you'd like to try—to give us a try—let me know. If not, tell me that instead and I'll back off. Either way, I'll respect your wishes."

He sounded so formal, so endearingly old-fashioned. His nearness, overwhelming and familiar at once, made her giddy. "I'd like to try."

The warmth of his smile felt like a reward. "I'm glad," he told her. He moved in close as though he meant to kiss her, but she held the envelope up like a flag.

Stopping in his tracks, he eyed her.

"Are you ready?" she asked, only the faintest quiver in her voice.

Despite the muscle clenching in his jaw, he nodded. "I guess so. Go ahead and open it."

Then it all came down to this. This moment, what—

ever was written on a small piece of paper, had the life-shattering capacity to change her world—their world.

Staring at the sealed envelope, heartbeat drumming in her ears, Emily finally shook her head. "I can't...." She shoved the results at him. "Here, you should be the one to open it."

To her surprise, though he held out his hand and accepted the envelope from her, he appeared reluctant. His blue eyes, full of trepidation, met hers before he nodded.

"Let's go into the kitchen," he said.

Emily followed him, the knot in her throat growing as he tore it open and extracted a piece of paper. As he began to read silently, his eyes narrowed, but otherwise his expression gave nothing away.

"Well?" she asked anxiously, reaching for the solid strength of his arm, unable to help herself. "What does it say?"

A cry of relief broke from his lips. "I'm the father. Ryan is my son."

Then, while Emily stood frozen, excitement and relief and fear all warring inside her, he swept her into his arms.

As he held her, a warm glow of peace and satisfaction came over her. His shoulders shook, and still he clung to her, obviously in the grip of strong emotion. With his hands locked behind her back, she held on, honored that he'd chosen to share this moment with her.

Finally, he raised his head. "Thank you," he said, his voice hoarse. "I meant what I said before. I won't take him away from you. But I'd still like to be part of yours and Ryan's life," he began, his deep voice simmering with emotion.

Inside her, everything stilled. She had to know, she

had to be sure. "Ryan will like that," she said, watching him, aware her heart shone in her eyes.

Taking a step closer, his eyes blazed with emotion. "What about you?" he asked. "Would you like that, too? Because Emily, I want to be with you and Ryan both—not one without the other."

A tentative happiness blossomed to life. "Are you sure?" she asked softly.

Crossing the room in three swift strides, he swept her into his arms and kissed her again. "Very sure."

Neither spoke for a long time after that.

* * * * *

**COMING NEXT MONTH from Harlequin®
Romantic Suspense**

AVAILABLE SEPTEMBER 18, 2012

#1723 THE COWBOY'S CLAIM
Cowboy Café
Carla Cassidy
When Nick's secret son is kidnapped, he and Courtney,
the woman he left behind, must work together to save him.

#1724 COLTON'S RANCH REFUGE
The Coltons of Eden Falls
Beth Cornelison
Movie star Violet Chastain witnesses an Amish girl's kidnapping,
so grumpy ex-soldier Gunnar Colton is assigned to protect
her—and babysit her rambunctious toddler twins.

#1725 CAVANAUGH'S SURRENDER
Cavanaugh Justice
Marie Ferrarella
A woman finds her sister dead and goes on a rampage to find
out the truth, running headlong into romance with the
investigating detective.

#1726 FLASH OF DEATH
Code X
Cindy Dees
With a dangerous drug cartel out to kill them both, can wild child
Trent break through the cold, cautious shell Chloe has erected
and find love?

You can find more information on upcoming Harlequin®
titles, free excerpts and more at www.Harlequin.com.

HRSCNM0912

REQUEST YOUR FREE BOOKS!
2 FREE NOVELS PLUS 2 FREE GIFTS!

ROMANTIC
SUSPENSE
Sparked by Danger, Fueled by Passion.

YES! Please send me 2 FREE Harlequin® Romantic Suspense novels and my 2 FREE gifts (gifts are worth about $10). After receiving them, if I don't wish to receive any more books, I can return the shipping statement marked "cancel." If I don't cancel, I will receive 4 brand-new novels every month and be billed just $4.49 per book in the U.S. or $5.24 per book in Canada. That's a saving of at least 14% off the cover price! It's quite a bargain! Shipping and handling is just 50¢ per book in the U.S. and 75¢ per book in Canada.* I understand that accepting the 2 free books and gifts places me under no obligation to buy anything. I can always return a shipment and cancel at any time. Even if I never buy another book, the two free books and gifts are mine to keep forever.

240/340 HDN FEFR

Name _____ (PLEASE PRINT)

Address _____ Apt. #

City _____ State/Prov. _____ Zip/Postal Code

Signature (if under 18, a parent or guardian must sign)

Mail to the **Reader Service:**

IN U.S.A.: P.O. Box 1867, Buffalo, NY 14240-1867
IN CANADA: P.O. Box 609, Fort Erie, Ontario L2A 5X3

Not valid for current subscribers to Harlequin Romantic Suspense books.

Want to try two free books from another line?
Call 1-800-873-8635 or visit www.ReaderService.com.

* Terms and prices subject to change without notice. Prices do not include applicable taxes. Sales tax applicable in N.Y. Canadian residents will be charged applicable taxes. Offer not valid in Quebec. This offer is limited to one order per household. All orders subject to credit approval. Credit or debit balances in a customer's account(s) may be offset by any other outstanding balance owed by or to the customer. Please allow 4 to 6 weeks for delivery. Offer available while quantities last.

Your Privacy—The Reader Service is committed to protecting your privacy. Our Privacy Policy is available online at www.ReaderService.com or upon request from the Reader Service.

We make a portion of our mailing list available to reputable third parties that offer products we believe may interest you. If you prefer that we not exchange your name with third parties, or if you wish to clarify or modify your communication preferences, please visit us at www.ReaderService.com/consumerchoice or write to us at Reader Service Preference Service, P.O. Box 9062, Buffalo, NY 14269. Include your complete name and address.

HRS11B

Out of the corner of her eye, she saw that the SUV was empty. Past it, near the trailhead, she glimpsed the beam of a flashlight bobbing as it headed down the trail.

The trail was wide and paved, and she found, once her eyes adjusted, that she didn't need to use her flashlight if she was careful. Enough starlight bled down through the pine boughs that she could see far enough ahead—she also knew the trail well.

There was no sign of Jordan, though. She'd reached the creek and bridge, quickly crossed it, and had started up the winding trail when she caught a glimpse of light above her on the trail.

She stopped to listen, afraid he might have heard her behind him. But there was only the sound of the creek and moan of the pines in the breeze. Somewhere in the distance, an owl hooted. She moved again, hurrying now.

Once the trail topped out, she should be able to see Jordan's light ahead of her, though she couldn't imagine what he was doing hiking to the falls tonight.

There was always a good chance of running into a moose or a wolf or, worse, this time of a year, a hungry grizzly foraging for food before hibernation.

The trail topped out. She stopped to catch her breath and listen for Jordan. Ahead she could make out the solid rock area at the base of the falls. A few more steps and she could feel the mist coming off the cascading water. From here, the trail carved a crooked path up through the pines to the top of the falls.

There was no sign of any light ahead and the only thing she could hear was the falls. Where was Jordan? She rushed on, convinced he was still ahead of her. Something rustled in the trees off to her right. A limb cracked somewhere ahead in the pines.

She stopped and drew her weapon. Someone was out there.

The report of the rifle shot felt so close it made the hair stand up on her neck. The sound ricocheted off the rock cliff and reverberated through her. Liza dived to the ground. A second shot echoed through the trees.

Weapon still drawn, she scrambled up the hill and almost tripped over the body Jordan Cardwell was standing over.

What was Jordan doing up at the falls so late at night? And is he guilty of more than just a walk in the moonlight?

Find out in the highly anticipated sequel
JUSTICE AT CARWELL RANCH
by USA TODAY *bestselling author*
B.J. Daniels.

Catch the thrill October 2, 2012.

HIEX1012

celebrating **15 YEARS**

Love Inspired® SUSPENSE

RIVETING INSPIRATIONAL ROMANCE

Another pulse-pounding story from miniseries

PROTECTION *Specialists*

As a trauma surgeon, Dr. Brenda Storm saves lives every day. But someone wants *her* dead. After an attempt on her life, the hospital hires a bodyguard to protect her 24/7. At first, Brenda doesn't think too-handsome Kyle Martin is right for the job. Then she discovers his harrowing background. With every attempt on her life, she's more drawn to the strong and silent man who risks his life for hers. But their growing feelings could put them *both* in harm's way.

THE DOCTOR'S DEFENDER

by fan-favorite author

Terri Reed

Available October 2012 wherever books are sold!

www.LoveInspiredBooks.com

HARLEQUIN  *Romance*

At their grandmother's request, three estranged
sisters return home for Christmas to the small town
of Beckett's Run. Little do they know that this family
reunion will reveal long-buried secrets…
and new-found love.

Discover the magic of Christmas in a brand-new
Harlequin® Romance miniseries.

In October 2012, find yourself
SNOWBOUND IN THE EARL'S CASTLE
by **Fiona Harper**

Be enchanted in November 2012 by a
SLEIGH RIDE WITH THE RANCHER
by **Donna Alward**

And be mesmerized in December 2012 by
MISTLETOE KISSES WITH THE BILLIONAIRE
by **Shirley Jump**

Available wherever books are sold.